TIME BINGE

Revised Edition, 2022.

ISBN: 978-0-9982120-1-2 (print)

ISBN: 978-0-9982120-0-5 (e-book)

Fonts: Plane Crash (licensed from WMKart.com), Garamond, Abadi MT Condensed Light.

Visit the author's website at www.martina-fetzer.com.

Cover by okdoodle.net. Edited by Ellen Campbell.

This is a work of fiction. Names, characters, places, and incidents either are the products of the author's imagination or are used fictitiously. Any resemblance to actual persons, living or dead, businesses, companies, events, or locales is entirely coincidental. Except Steve Buscemi. Resemblance to Steve Buscemi is intentional.

TIME BINGE

⁂

MARTINA FETZER

TABLE OF CONTENTS

CONTENT NOTE

This series is meant to be funny. Many of the characters have traumatic backgrounds and gruesome events sometimes happen, but none of these are described very graphically. That being said, content warnings for each book in the series are available at the author's website: martina-fetzer.com.

For Steve Buscemi

PROLOGUE

Those who are paid to say such things say that opening a novel with a prologue is a bad idea. Patience Cloyce had never heard that advice. Other things she had never heard of included commercial deodorant (invented in 1888) and the notion of women's suffrage (still controversial today). All of that is to say that Patience was a Puritan living in Salem, Massachusetts. The year was 1692 and the mood was becoming tense. Accusations of witchcraft abounded and the fifteen-year-old wandered miserably around the forest behind her parents' homestead in an effort to walk off the unfortunate case of hiccups that had befallen her. One of her closest friends, Sarah, had been hanged for sneezing forty-two times in a row—the result of some poorly timed seasonal allergies—and Patience hoped to avoid a similar biological function-related death sentence. She was lucky enough that she hadn't been killed for having fiery red hair.

HIRP! They still weren't gone.

HIRP HIRUP! She glanced at the familiar surroundings: a tree, a slightly larger tree, a felled tree, a tree stump, a shrub that resembled a small tree... all of this was mundane. While it was certainly in her best interest to stay out of trouble—HIRP—she'd had her fill of trees and treelike plants and decided to venture farther into the forest. She grabbed a branch to use as a walking stick and defiantly passed the crooked dogwood that marked the end of her family's property. HIRP!

There she found more trees. As it turned out, there was little else in the forests of seventeenth-century Massachusetts. She had imagined there would be new creatures, new streams, maybe even a new species of tree; however, those hopes were mistaken. Everything was hiccups and trees. Still, it was beautiful, and a good place to think (God help her if she were caught thinking in public).

HIRP. After she had walked about half a mile from home, she sat down on the edge of a large log and began contemplating her existence. As soon as she did, a wayward branch that had wedged itself underneath the log scraped her ankle. Bleeding on a log in the middle of an unknown expanse of forest just about summed up her existence so far.

Had she been born a few hundred years later, Patience might have been a feminist. She did, after all, prefer felt hats to bonnets and oversized belt buckles to aprons. Had she been born a few hundred years later, she would have taken to her blog and written a lengthy diatribe, then been distracted by a 'Which Fictional Vampire Would You Totally Sleep With?' quiz and given up on the whole endeavor. Had she been born a few hundred years earlier, on the other hand, she would have died of Bubonic Plague. As it was, she was only capable of sitting on a log thinking *life isn't fair.* Because she was a Puritan, she immediately felt ashamed for thinking it.

It was true, though. Life wasn't fair. In addition to the late Sarah Good, there were Giles Corey (pressed to death for singing a hymn in the wrong key), Alice Parker (hanged for baking a particularly bad blackberry pie), and Ann Pudeator (hanged for allegedly turning into a bird). Nobody had a good explanation for why Ann didn't fly from the noose. And those were just the people Patience personally knew. There were probably twenty others murdered by the mob for offenses ranging from flying via broomstick to owning a black cat. Salem, Massachusetts was a terrible place to live and, with no sign of the trials ending, Patience had run out of her name. HIRP.

"God help me," she prayed aloud, squelching her final hiccup.

God, as it turns out, wasn't listening at the moment. Well,

her god wasn't listening. The demigods from Alpha Centauri who call themselves something that cannot be spelled but sounds approximately like kn'saw-yah-poutines were most certainly listening. But it wasn't the poutines who orchestrated her escape from a dull, tree-filled existence. As she stood, preparing to make the short walk home, a gust of wind blew a piece of brilliant white paper across her path. The crumpled note settled in right in front of her, wedging itself in a tree branch. Having never seen 92 bright copy paper from Staples, her curiosity was piqued. Patience knelt down, picked it up, and read it three times to determine that it really didn't make any sense:

I can't do this anymore. I'm sorry, Stan.
- Hudson Marrow

1 / MORE PAPER

Somewhere beneath lower Manhattan, voices were raised.
Just one voice, actually. It belonged to Edward Smith, a crag-
gly, late-thirties blond with a demeanor as surly as his name
was common.

"I don't give a shit. You wanna know how many less shits
I could give?" Smith asked, tossing a scrap of 92 bright copy
paper into the trash by way of a small plastic basketball hoop.

"Fewer," his partner corrected. Arturo Brooks was a few
years younger than Smith, and more than a few degrees tan-
ner and cuter.

The paper bounced off a growing mound of paper and
landed on the floor, defiant.

"What?" Smith asked.

"Shits are countable, so..."

"*Fine*. You want to know how many... fewer... shits I could
give?"

Brooks sighed. "How many?"

Smith glowered at the paper ball. "None. None... fewer
shits." He groaned. "Momentum's gone. Thanks."

He did, in fact, give a shit about missing the net. Things he
didn't give a shit about included the difference between 'less'
and 'fewer' and the mission he and his partner had just been
handed. Agents Brooks and Smith were paranormal detectives when circumstances permitted, and they had been
tasked with investigating a missing persons report. After thirteen years of service to the Reticent, Smith felt the task was
beneath him. Brooks made the point that refusing another
job could get him fired, which prompted the aforewritten
lack of shit giving.

Smith rolled his hole-ridden office chair closer to Brooks
and looked him straight in the eyes. "You remember when

we used to hunt vampires or stop mystic cults?"

"No," Brooks answered dryly. "It completely slipped my mind."

"What happened to—"

"We got old," Brooks said, echoing every buddy cop film he'd ever seen. Among his favorite movies were *Lethal Weapon*, *Lethal Weapon 2*, and *Lethal Wet Fun* (a pornographic parody). He'd never met a cliché he didn't love.

Smith rolled his eyes and continued griping. "We're in our thirties, not dead. Fucking missing persons reports." He threw his novelty toilet-shaped coffee mug at the wall, where it shattered loudly. The pieces slid down a pile of multicolored mug shrapnel with a series of gentle clinks. With each day, the amount of trash on the floor of their office grew. Brooks would have complained, but there was no reasoning with Smith when he was like this, which is to say there was no reasoning with him at all. He was always like this.

"And *why isn't there a janitor anymore?*" Smith complained, staring at the heap. There was a janitor; he just refused to service their office after encountering too many dubious substances. "This whole place is run by idiots. Hell, I could do a better job and *I'm* an idiot."

Brooks remained patient as his partner's rant continued.

"We saved this whole goddamn city from the Goblin King..." Smith said.

That was true. Upon learning about the prophecy of Klakon and the inevitable rise of the Goblin King that would plunge the world into total darkness, suspicion turned to David Bowie. Agents Brooks and Smith were the ones who determined that it was Steve Buscemi all along. They appropriately ended his reign of terror by shoving him into a woodchipper. The actor who purports to be Steve Buscemi to this day is a changeling who owed the two men a favor. It was the stuff of legend. Then again, a lot of what went on within the Reticent was stuff of legend, if you were to ask someone on the street. Actually, if you were to ask someone on the street about the Goblin King, they would just ignore you and assume you were insane, especially in Manhattan. Still, Brooks and Smith's Goblin King assassination was the stuff of legend in an organization for which it took something special to earn the moniker "stuff of legend."

Despite their well-earned fame, it was the opinion of Charlotte Nguyen, their immediate superior of three months, that Brooks and Smith were no longer fit for such perilous adventures. It was her opinion because it was her superior's opinion and his superior's above him. People like Agent Nguyen, in their attempts to climb the corporate ladder, rarely had opinions of their own. Having heard the sound of yet another mug meeting its demise, she threw open the door to their office.

"Is there a problem?" she asked.

Smith rose from his office chair, which itself rose a little in relief of his weight.

"Sure is," he said.

"Eddie..." Brooks pleaded from his seat.

"What's with the shit jobs?" Smith asked accusingly.

"Watch your tone." Nguyen looked from Smith to Brooks and back. "They're no 'shittier' than the jobs anyone else is getting. Paranormal activity is at an all-time low. That's all."

Smith tilted his head in disbelief. "Really? There's nothing happening in New York City? Nine million people and not a werewolf or a wight in sight? We're supposed to believe that?"

Brooks cringed, mostly at his partner's accidental rhyme.

"Really. But if you keep kicking up a fuss we can make 'Agents Brooks and Smith Fired' a thing that's happening."

"Talking back to you isn't grounds for firing," Smith said. If disrespecting superiors had been a serious violation, he'd have been fired a decade ago.

Nguyen smiled smugly. "No, but intraoffice romance is."

Smith's lip curled.

The relationship between Agents Brooks and Smith was one of the worst-kept secrets among the Reticent, and it would have gotten many other agents fired years earlier. For this reason, Smith called his boss's bluff with a quip. "I know you're not over our torrid affair, Charlotte, but I didn't think you'd ever tattle."

She scowled. There was a lot of scowling in this office.

When silence followed, Brooks seized the opportunity to change subjects. "Is anyone looking into *why* there's not much activity happening?"

"No, it never crossed my mind," Nguyen said, glaring at him. "I'm building a team for just that. Look into the missing persons report, then come back here and we'll talk about putting you two on it."

As she turned to face the door, Smith looked at Brooks and broke into an exaggerated grin.

She addressed them once more as she reached for the doorknob. "And quit throwing mugs against the wall, would you?"

"I make no promises," Smith said.

"Well, fix your tie and get out of here." With that, she walked off, her heels click-clacking against ancient linoleum.

When Agent Nguyen was completely out of earshot, Brooks took to scolding Smith. "Do you want to get us fired? We could be retired in twenty years and I, for one, don't feel like starting a new career in my thirties."

Smith shifted uncomfortably, as he always did when Brooks talked about the future, then covered his discomfort with sarcasm, as he always did when anyone talked about anything. "Only twenty years? Whew! We're just days away." He sat back down—his chair complained with a squeak—and moved toward his partner, rolling his chair as hard as was humanly possible. "I remember when you were fun."

"I remember when you knew when to shut up."

"That's a lie. That never happened," said Smith. He inched closer. "They haven't fired us in seven years, and you know as well as I do they've known the whole time." It was, after all, the Reticent's job to know everything. Smith's chair bumped into Brooks's and he leaned back, practically onto his partner's lap. "We're too good at this shit."

"Too good at solving missing persons reports?" Brooks wondered.

Smith shrugged. "The best."

"Do you believe the things that come out of your mouth?" Brooks asked, looking down at him.

"Mostly," Smith said. "Do you believe the people who come into your mouth?"

Brooks rolled his eyes as hard as was humanly possible. Smith grabbed the back of Brooks's head and pulled him down for a brief kiss. The younger man let his lips hover over Smith's for just a moment as he blindly corrected Smith's tie; then he grabbed the back of the chair and rolled his partner away. He stood up, grabbed his coat from the back of his own chair, and motioned for the door.

"*Fiiiine.*" Smith grabbed his investigative kit—a plain brown briefcase—and headed for the door. "Missing persons report," he sneered, shutting it behind him.

2 / SHE'S A WITCH

Time is non-linear,* so while Agents Brooks and Smith were busy making their way to Staten Island to investigate the mysterious disappearance of a Mr. Hudson Marrow, Patience Cloyce was busy telling her parents about the strange letter she had found in the woods. Unfortunately for her, Bartholomew and Prudence Cloyce's ties to their community were much stronger than their ties to the second youngest of their nine children. Middle children of the twenty-first century think they have it bad when they're overshadowed by the accomplishments of older siblings and the cuteness of younger ones, but there is no position worse than eighth of nine.

There was a lingering, uncomfortable silence before her father finally spoke.

"You created this, didn't you?" he asked, holding up the note.

"No, sir," she insisted. "I found it, like I told you."

"That's nonsense. No one has ever seen paper like this before."

"That's why I brought it to you immediately," Patience said. It was at this point that she realized what a terrible mistake she'd made. She was being interrogated over a piece of paper.

"What does it mean?" Bartholomew asked, pointing an accusing finger her way.

"I don't know what it means, sir. I found it and brought it home in hopes that you might know," Patience said.

Her father shook his head in disappointment. "First you go into the forest alone. You say you were out there *thinking*. Then you bring back a piece of paper that tells of Satan."

---

* And prologues are not optional.

"Father, I believe it says 'Stan'..." She wasn't the most literate person in town, but she was certain she could tell the difference.

"Quiet!" he demanded. It wasn't that Bartholomew Cloyce couldn't tell the difference between Satan and Stan; it was that he was just as caught up in the witch hysteria as anyone. "It's obviously a spelling mistake. You're no stupider than the average girl your age. Surely you must know how this looks to others—how our family will be seen."

"No?" It was at that moment Patience felt *a lot* stupider than most girls her age. She had taken great care to avoid being seen walking in the woods or hiccuping in front of anyone, but she assumed that if anyone could be trusted to discuss the letter from the forest it would be her parents. After all, they had only been present for two of the last seven hangings and they had chosen the smallest stone available when it was time to help press Mr. Corey to death.

Her father made a declaration: "I will not have this witchcraft in my home."

He said the W word. Her heart sank. Patience knew that she was, in impolite modern terms, screwed. In order to avoid the appearance of being soft on witchcraft, her father brought her to the town magistrate. There, as she walked the dull grey stone path toward the dull grey building through dull grey fog, Patience made a decision. She would plead guilty. She would plead guilty because any plea would lead to being hanged, pressed, or—if the townspeople were feeling particularly wild—burnt to a crisp. A guilty plea would at least save her the anguish of months in jail eating tree bark and a drawn-out trial.

Her thoughts centered around the word stupid: *Stupid witches. Stupid world. Stupid paper. Stupid, sinful me being negative.*

The second hardest part of being a Puritan was the emotional self-flagellation. The hardest, of course, was the inevitable horrific death. If it didn't happen via a noose, it would happen later during the birth of anywhere from her first to sixteenth child (sixteen was the furthest anyone in Salem had made it before dying). Patience shuddered. Having witnessed seven hangings and the birth of her newest niece, she found the former to be far less traumatic.

At least I won't pass in childbirth, she thought. *That's positive. Positive thinking is good.*

Realizing she held a negative view of one of God's miracles, she prayed for forgiveness. By the time the unpleasant business with the magistrate was over, she had prayed six times and thought the word 'positive' over thirty seven. Neither helped her cause. Nor did her calm, rational explanation of how she had come to possess a piece of 92 bright copy paper that bore the devil's name. The lack of spelling standardization, rampant illiteracy, and witchcraft panic combined to convince everyone who could read the letter that Stan was, in fact, Satan.

Patience was sentenced to be hanged, and the piece of 92 bright copy paper was sentenced to be burned.* When the Salem magistrate handed out a sentence, it was handed out swiftly. He marshaled the young girl out of the courtroom and into the street almost immediately.

While the streets of Salem, Massachusetts in 1692 had never been particularly kind, Patience's memories of them were nonetheless fond. Before all this witchcraft nonsense, there had been a real sense of community in Salem. There still was, of course, but she had been cast out from that community. She passed by the stocks where her childhood friend Creedence had once been left for four days following youthful antics at the apple orchard. While the thought of those

---

* This was not the strangest sentencing in Salem. At one point, a head of cabbage had been sentenced to be ripped to shreds and fed to the local rabbits. That was the most violent punishment they had ever conceived, if the sentience of cabbage can be presupposed.

days would have normally made her smile, she frowned. She was being hanged, after all.

The gallows were unpleasant. Instead of the type of rigging that instantly broke a person's neck when they fell, the people of Salem intentionally built their gallows to be ineffective and painful. Jeremiah Cutwright, the last person to be hanged, had taken over an hour to asphyxiate. As she ascended the creaking staircase, Patience thought about the choking sounds he'd made. Sarah died in only twelve minutes, though, so perhaps she would have similar luck. She thought about how strange it was to wish for a swift death. She also thought about how positively stupid she had been, then prayed for forgiveness. After all, God had made her perfect and God wouldn't make a stupid girl, unless it was for a reason.

Everyone in town had gathered for the hanging. It was impressive considering that she'd only been sentenced fifteen minutes earlier. Then again, there wasn't much to watch in Salem other than executions, and keeping up appearances was of the utmost importance. When the hanging bell rang, citizens scurried to get the best spots.

Gathered up front were Patience's parents, who simply shook their heads and tutted, unfazed by the impending death of their least significant child. They were surrounded by her siblings, who may have been sad but didn't dare show it. Patience was a witch, they reasoned, and witches had to be killed.

"Do you have any last words?" the hooded hangman asked as he slipped the noose around her neck. She recognized his voice as that of her neighbor John Wilmington and silently cursed his betrayal.

In her situation, last words would have been utterly futile, so Patience shook her head.

Life isn't fair.

The floor dropped, and she shook her head more and more violently as she struggled to breathe. The crowd cheered for several minutes as Patience died in agony.

Then something peculiar happened. Patience woke up.

3 / THE DAY THE MOON STOOD STILL

Human beings first landed on the moon in 1969, but it wasn't until the two hundredth anniversary of that occasion that human beings settled the moon. They could have done it a few decades sooner, but then the colonization would have lost symbolic value. Originally, the settlers numbered only in the dozens. Their purpose was to maintain a facility that built and launched shuttles farther into space. With the help of a few enormous 3D printers for manufacturing, it was cheaper to launch shuttles from Luna's low surface gravity than to launch them from Earth.

After a few decades, its exclusivity led Luna to become home to many of the most pretentious Earthlings. Portland, Oregon's population fell by 500,000 between 2180 and 2200, and it wasn't uncommon to hear Lunans say, "There's just no doubt that the food here is locally sourced" or "I've been brewing my own beer with lunar hops."

The colony worked like this: the moon's surface held a series of domes that hosted the crops necessary for sustaining life as well as the machinery necessary for maintaining those crops. Would it have been easier to simply print food? Yes, but Lunans wouldn't have anything to do with GMOs. Connecting the farms were a complex series of underground buildings that housed Luna's citizens and shielded them from solar radiation and moon dust. It was in those tunnels that several generations of hipsters didn't merely survive but thrived, becoming the underground they so dearly loved.

It was also in those tunnels that Lemon Jones sat bored in class, scribbling ancient album covers on her notebook as her 11th grade teacher, Ms. Krump, called roll. It was only a minute into her first class on the first day of the school year and Lemon had almost finished drawing the black glove on The Strokes' *Is This It*. While her eyes ignored everything but her art, her ears took in the rollcall.

"Ark'meedees... Bonanzaw... Ballaiden... Crhyjylan..."

Lemon lamented her strange name. When it was called, there were a few chuckles around the room. She hurriedly raised her hand, then lowered it to add the text to her album cover.

"Minystree... Moon Unit... Nicholas..."

Luna's grey jumpsuit school uniforms were supposed to reduce bullying, but upon hearing that name—one even more bizarre than Lemon's—the students broke into uproarious laughter at its bearer's expense. The new student, a transfer from Earth's Florida, blushed.

"*Nicholas?*" a classmate scoffed.

Ms. Krump attempted to settle the teenagers down, but she had to wait out the laughter. She couldn't help but chuckle a little to herself. Her own name was 3! and she hadn't known anyone with a name like Nicholas in her lifetime. By the time the laughter settled, Lemon had moved on to Neutral Milk Hotel's *In An Aeroplane Over the Sea*. It wasn't that she didn't care about her education. It was that she already knew all of the history Ms. Krump intended to teach. Lunan public education catered to the lowest common denominator, and Lemon had heard the same stories of World Wars I, II, and III over and over again. By eleventh grade, she was simply biding her time.

While the teacher droned on about her low expectations for the semester, there was a sudden knock on the classroom door. Lemon looked up, and her eyes met the familiar face of her older brother, Tangelo. At 6'5" he towered over most Lunans (they were a sickly people), but his height was especially comical next to the tiny Ms. Krump. Lemon was more amused by this than she was concerned at the reason her brother had come to retrieve her from school only minutes after it had begun.

Tangelo whispered something to the teacher, presented her with an official-looking piece of paper, and the announcement was made: "Lemon, you are excused."

She scooped her notebook into the backpack under her desk and bolted. In the corridors of Luna, Lemon dutifully followed her brother.

"Where are we going?" she asked. "Tell me it's exciting."

"Work." Tangelo's response was terse, as most of his responses were. It was with good reason. All Lunans faced conscription upon reaching their 21st birthdays. He had just celebrated his 21st birthday, and his caregiving waiver would soon run out when Lemon turned 18.

"Work's not exciting." Lemon came to a halt and put her hands on her hips. "You took me out of school to help you do your job?"

He stopped and turned to her. "No." He didn't want to say anything to worry his sister, but there was cause for worry. He simply tugged her forward. "You'll see when we get there."

Noticing his hurried pace, Lemon began to worry anyway. She kept this to herself. Any time she showed the slightest sign of distress, Tangelo turned into Concerned Older Brother™. While it was somewhat sweet and certainly necessary in the aftermath of their parents' deaths, she preferred the Cool Older Brother™ who gave her a little breathing room.

The corridors under the moon's surface—normally filled with pompous chatter and the guitar strumming of the willfully unemployed—were eerily quiet, and Lemon became acutely aware of her own footsteps. Clack clack clack. CLACK. There was no silencing her moonoak-soled clogs as they approached the central tunnel that housed Luna's most important officials. Tangelo's finger and irises were scanned, and he was cleared to proceed. They filled out a visitor's form for Lemon.

"Destination?" Lemon asked, typing her information onto a tablet.

"The Office of the President," Tangelo said.

She tilted her head and stared for a good thirty seconds. Definitely cause for worry.

President Sanford's office was terribly disorganized. That was no surprise. Lemon had never been there before, but she'd heard plenty of Tangelo's stories. As the President's personal aide (read: intern), he had witnessed a lot. Lemon's favorite story was the one in which the President tripped over a stapler—not because it was funny that the President tripped (it was), but because she loved her mind's picture of the kind of chaotic office that would have a stapler on the floor.

Reality very nearly matched her expectations. What she didn't expect was that the room would also look like a child's bedroom from the 1970s. The wood-paneled walls were covered in *Star Wars* posters and Spirograph drawings and there was a chalkboard where their leader had scribbled some smiley faces and peace signs. The second her eyes noticed the Raggedy Ann doll in the corner of the room, Lemon became politically concerned for the first time. She didn't want someone this immature running her home satellite, however cool his collection of retro goods may have been.

Nevertheless, when she heard President Sanford clear his throat, she stood at attention and refrained from commenting. Childish as he may have been, he was the President.

President Sanford was tall enough to have been imposing, but pudgy and poor-postured enough not to be. He brushed his long, blond hair away from his sun-deprived face and pulled it into a man bun.

"Are you ready?" he asked.

"Yes, sir," Tangelo answered.

"This way, then," the President said.

Lemon whispered to her brother as they followed the President into the next room. "What's going on?"

As if on cue, an explosion rocked the corridor outside. One of the framed spirographs fell from the wall, cracking its frame. Tangelo's pace turned to a rush, and Lemon mimicked it, pausing only for a second to grab the vintage spirograph and stuff it into her backpack.

"What's. Going. On?" she asked as they approached a large lump covered with a black sheet—about the size and shape of a craft beer fermentation tank.

President Sanford ripped away the emperor-sized sheet to reveal a metal capsule reminiscent of a cartoon spaceship. It was a modest pod that could comfortably fit three, four if one of those people weren't the portly President. As one of them was said President, it fit three.

"Come on," President Sanford said.

"It's another terrorist attack or something," Tangelo said as they boarded the device.

Lemon inspected the inside of the pod, which appeared to consist of a 1950s diner booth and some comically oversized knobs. For good measure, the booth also featured the keypad from a TI-30 calculator. The President tapped away at it.

"This is a bomb shelter?" Lemon asked, hesitantly taking a seat in the booth.

"In a sense," President Sanford said.

"Who's attacking us?" she asked.

"Hold on," Tangelo directed.

There were no state fairs on the moon (or states, for that matter), but if there had been, Lemon would have been reminded of the Gravitron ride—the one where passengers stick to the wall thanks to centrifugal force. She soon found herself stuck to the back of the diner booth as the pod began to spin. The ensuing dizziness and sudden flashing green light brought her thoughts to a halt. Lemon simply shut her eyes and attempted not to puke.

She puked.

4 / STATEN ISLAND SUCKS

It's easy to forget that Staten Island is a borough of New York City and not, as is often believed, a receptacle for its human waste. Reticent agents passed around assignments on Staten Island like roofied drinks at a frat party—the kind of frat party that could be encountered at a community college on Staten Island. One agent, Derick Giovanni, reacted to receiving an assignment there by jumping off the Staten Island ferry and neglecting to keep himself afloat. Admittedly, he had been going through a tough time on account of the divorce and losing custody of his daughter, but it is believed that Staten Island was the last straw. It is believed because his suicide note contained only three words: "Staten Island sucks."

Those words repeated in the minds of Agents Brooks and Smith as they boarded that same ferry. Could the Reticent have teleported them to their destination? Certainly. Would they spare the expense? Not a chance. Even when paranormal business was booming, they were stingy with travel reimbursement. Since the averted apocalypse in December 2012, things had only gotten worse. The world was a safer place, but safety was bad for business. Company cards had been cut off. The cafeteria had switched to a low-cost, low-effort food supplier. Employees were encouraged to work in almost total darkness to save on electric costs. There was hardly an agent around who hadn't tried to find a new employer, but career opportunities for people with the skillset of staking vampires, vanquishing demons, and mulching the Goblin King Steve Buscemi were obviously limited.

Brooks sighed the heaviest of sighs.

Smith sometimes had difficulty interpreting the immense variety of sighs that came out of his partner's mouth. He wagered that this one was more sad than it was annoyed, and he sought confirmation. "Staten Island?"

Brooks exhaled slowly. "Staten Island."

Those were the only two words he needed to say. The pair had always found an excuse not to take assignments on Staten Island, and Brooks hadn't been there in nearly a decade for good reason.

"Sorry," Smith said. While he generally had a heart three times smaller than the Grinch's at its smallest, he meant it.

Staten Island's Willowbrook Park was where the two men first met ten years earlier. It was where an attack by an undead horde left only one survivor—Brooks—and where he was recruited by a man six years his senior to help make sure it never happened again. Despite it having been the impetus for their relationship, they rarely talked about it because that would be, in Smith's own words, "super gay." Because certain childhood experiences had, again in his own words, "fucked him up beyond belief," Smith hated anything remotely resembling the sharing of feelings. Just the thought of continuing this conversation made him want to buy some lumber, drink some whiskey, and listen to Motorhead.

While Smith tried to make himself feel more toxically masculine, Brooks was busy experiencing trauma of his own. The ferry prepared to dock and he could see the low-income housing where his father had raised him and his twin sister, Tasha. He closed his eyes and muttered "fuck" to himself. Unlike Smith, Brooks wasn't big on cursing, but when an attack struck he couldn't help it—nor could he help switching from English to Spanish and back in his angst. Flashes of grey and crimson filled his mind. Then there was the piercing sound of a final, deathly holler.

He continued, "fuck fuck, *dios me impida saltar de este barco.*" Brooks was acutely aware of his propensity for panic attacks, and he had been careful about avoiding Staten Island because of them. His therapist called it anticipatory anxiety brought on by post-traumatic stress; Smith called it "fuck mode." Whatever the phrasing, Brooks buried his head in his shaking hands, still murmuring. "*Prefiero chingar a un pato que estar aquí,* fuck fuck—"

Smith pushed his inner critic to the back of his mind and put a hand on his partner's shoulder. "We can turn around if you want."

"No," Brooks snipped, brushing him away. "If we bail on this one, we'll never get another good assignment." He could practically feel the thick blood splashing against his face. "Fuck," he breathed.

"To hell with the job," Smith said.

Brooks forced himself to speak through a tightened throat. "You were just telling Charlotte—"

"Yeah, and now I'm telling you: to hell with it. It's not worth it if you end up drooling in a padded room. If you want out, I'll mop floors for the next twenty years."

"I'll be fine," Brooks insisted, stifling his impulse to vomit.

"You sure?" Smith asked. Due to circumstances, he knew more than a few people whose entire families had been wiped out by wraiths, and none of them were ever "fine."

"Yeah, let's go." Brooks stood up and wobbled back and forth for a moment before immediately dropping to the deck, unconscious. He was not fine.

*
**

Brooks found himself in the backseat of a running cab with a stinging pain in his left thigh and no idea where he was. When his sense of smell awoke and picked up nothing but menthol and body odor, he began piecing it together. Then he saw the cab driver standing outside the front passenger door smoking a cigarette and, unable to get the door handle to work, he tapped on the glass to get the man's attention.

At least he got a cab, Brooks thought. His father had been a cab driver, and every time someone insisted on using a rideshare instead of a taxi, Brooks broke into a lengthy diatribe about medallions and scab labor. It was tedious for everyone involved.

"Where am I?" he asked as the driver obliged his exit.

The driver tossed his cigarette onto a pile of butts on the ground. "Staten Island."

"Oh," Brooks said. He stared at his hand for a moment, concerned that it was steady. While he still felt like he could puke, the sense of dread was gone. When he coupled that with the fact that his leg was still burning, he knew exactly what had happened and silently cursed his partner.

Outside the cab, there was a garbage bin. Due to the character of local residents, it was pristine while the trash that should have filled it covered the sidewalk. Brooks leaned on that immaculate bin, head spinning. He had a feeling that, if he tried to walk, he would fall over.

"Where's Eddie?" he asked.

"Who?"

"The guy who told you to watch me," Brooks said. "Where is he?"

"In there." The driver pointed at the set of brand-new condos across the street.

Across the street isn't far, Brooks thought. He thanked the driver, un-leaned from the garbage bin, and stumbled off the curb to cross the street. His slow hobble didn't get him far before he was interrupted.

"Hey!" the driver shouted, interrupting the graceless display.

Brooks sighed yet again. Of course Smith hadn't paid the fare. What little goodwill he had garnered by using a proper taxi was fading.

"How much?" Brooks asked, now leaning on the back of the cab.

"$35," said the driver.

Brooks pulled two twenties from his wallet, paid the man who seemed insulted at only receiving a 14% tip, then continued stumbling toward the building.

Whoever their missing person Hudson Marrow was, he had a fair amount of money. The building was possibly the nicest on Staten Island (granted, that's not saying much). Apartment 157 was their assignment, and after showing the doorman a fake NYPD badge, Brooks made his way there without much difficulty. The door was already cracked open, so he went inside for an enthusiastic welcome.

"Look at this shit!" Smith said, feigning enthusiasm.

"Did you *drug* me?" Brooks asked, changing the subject.

"I did, but look at this," Smith said, changing it back. He tossed a blueprint to his partner and awaited a reaction as strong as the one he'd just put on.

Smith already knew that time machines existed. He'd known that for ten years now. But Brooks didn't know that he knew, and due to paradoxes or some boring shit like that Smith had to keep it that way. It was one Reticent rule that seemed worth following.

Brooks squinted at the paper. The blueprint appeared to be the plan for one such time machine, as the top of the blueprint was labeled 'Time Machine' and below that was a drawing of an unassuming time machine. It was square at the bottom and narrowed to a point at the top, like a cartoon spaceship. To the right of that, there was a drawing of interior knobs and levers that were attached to an old 1950s diner booth.

"Ugly," Smith complained. "So this guy, Hudson Marrow—"

Brooks stared at the blueprint. "Just because he has a gag blueprint doesn't mean he discovered time travel."

"Look around, babe."

In his immediate and rightful need to chastise Smith for sticking him with a dose of Valium, Brooks had failed to look carefully around the room. When he finally did, he was stunned. The apartment seemed to belong to a time-traveling hoarder. A quellazaire from the 1920s sat atop a Buddhist holy text, which sat next to an Aztec feather shield. There were three very different suits of armor, Civil War rifles, ancient Indian jewelry, an original piece by Monet (not that either Brooks or Smith recognized it as such), piles of Viking coins, African tribal masks, and so on. All of it crammed into a 900 square foot apartment. Like both men's youths, it was a beautiful disaster.

"Explains how he could afford the apartment," Brooks said. Hudson Marrow was, according to his brief research, a community college professor. While an admirable enough career, it wouldn't afford this apartment, even on Staten Island.

Smith focused on the one item in the room that wasn't an antique: a skull-shaped cigarette lighter (approximate retail value: USD $9.87). He scanned the room and, content that Brooks was looking at everything but him, pocketed it. He was just in time.

"Hey, look at this," Brooks said, turning his eyes to his partner. He approached holding a picture of two people: Hudson Marrow and a woman who was presumably his mother at game four of the Stanley Cup Finals. "He looks like you."

"What?" Smith glanced at the photo and gestured the idea away. "No he doesn't. He's fat."

"Well he's your fat twin." It was an exaggeration, but Smith and Hudson did look remarkably similar: short blonde hair, bulging green eyes and taut lips that refused to put up with anyone's bullshit photography. They could easily have been brothers.

"Wait a minute," Smith said, remembering something he had not actually read but had scanned briefly. "According to his file, he's fifty years old. He looks younger than I do."

"Well, you have lived a hard life—"

"Shut up," Smith said.

Brooks gave the photo another look. Smith's point was a valid one. Hudson appeared to be thirty at most. "Huh. You think he took the time machine here from the future or something? Skipped the early 2000s? I wouldn't blame him..."

"I don't know, but I don't like it."

"Maybe he's future you," Brooks mocked, "coming back to tell you to not eat so much."

Smith rolled his eyes. "Maybe he's future me coming back to tell me to break up with you."

They continued browsing the apartment's artifacts as they made their way to Hudson's bedroom. Brooks was a window shopper, thinking it rude to rifle through someone else's things, even if they were stolen from the past. Smith, on the other hand, didn't give a second's thought to Hudson Marrow; he thrusted every sword, typed at every typewriter, and massaged every lump of clay. There was only one, but he still made sure he formed it into a crude phallic shape as he passed.

In contrast to the rest of the apartment, the bedroom was tidy. The bed was made, no clothes were strewn about, and it had the pleasant smell of a blueberry candle rather than the thrift store odor that emanated through the rest of the apartment. The only thing of note was the obvious time machine in the corner. It was a metallic pod about seven feet high and five feet wide—partly covered by a king-sized black sheet.

"Gee, think we found it?" Smith asked.

"*Honestly.* Why even bother trying to hide it?"

Smith pretended to be their missing person. "Surely nobody will notice my giant time machine if I cover it with a sheet." He scoffed in contempt. "Idiot."

Brooks pulled away the sheet and, sure enough, it looked just like the blueprint: sleek on the outside and boxy on the inside with mechanical parts that neither Brooks nor Smith was capable of understanding.

"Yep, that's our time machine," Brooks assessed.

"Kinda shitty, isn't it?" Smith asked, eyeing the teal diner booth that made up the time machine's seating.

"Yeah, but I mean... that's a time machine."

It took a moment for the realization to hit. This was big. Brooks ran a hand down the side of the pod, thinking about everything this one object might be able to change. Could they undo anything they regretted? Save anyone they'd failed to save? Reveal future perils that might befall them? This was big. There wasn't a synonym for 'big' big enough to describe this level of big. It was big.

"I wonder how it works," he said.

"You're the scientist. You tell me," Smith snarked.

As it turns out, 96 credit hours toward a bachelor's in chemistry did not qualify Brooks to explain time travel. He shrugged. "I've got nothing."

"You want to call it in or have me do it?" Smith asked.

Brooks paused while he thought up a suitably snide response. "Why don't you do it? I'm afraid I'm too drugged to form a coherent sentence."

Smith was going to get so big an earful later that no q-tip could save him. But Brooks was merely mad at him, not completely freaking out like he had been on the ferry. He could work with mad.

While Brooks continued fondling and pondering the time machine, Smith called Agent Nguyen.

"Yeah, we found something," he said into the phone. "Code Fourteen..." A shout from the other end of the line was so loud it caused Brooks to turn as Smith continued, "No, I'm not kidding."

5 / MORE TREES

The room was dark, a consequence of it being a) night time, and b) a few centuries before the advent of in-home electricity. Patience fumbled around the dirt floor, feeling for anything that seemed familiar. No such luck. There was nothing but dirt, dirt, and more dirt. She longed for anything else, even if it had to be a tree.

The undertaker was her savior. When he entered the room holding a lantern, she finally got a good look at her surroundings and stood up. Unfortunately, getting a good look at her surroundings meant getting a good look at two fly-swarmed corpses in the corner, both unrecognizable in death. She remembered that she too was supposed to be a corpse, and panicked. She realized that she was wearing nothing but her undergarments and panicked harder. The undertaker panicked hardest of all; the sight of the dead girl springing to life caused him to have a heart attack and fall to the floor in her place. His lantern tumbled but miraculously landed right side up, still lit.

"Sir?" she asked, backing away from him to look for her clothes. Even if he was having a heart attack, she couldn't come closer and expose herself to the man in her current state.

The undertaker failed to respond. He twitched for a few seconds and fell still, joining the room's other occupants in death. A few anxious flies took notice and flew his way. Patience breathed deeply and tried not to be terrified. She'd seen plenty of deaths, of course. Everyone in Salem had. She'd never seen anyone spring back to life, though, and judging from the undertaker's reaction, he hadn't either. She had no idea what was happening to her and she had no desire to be unprecedented—her Lord and savior notwithstanding.

In the dim light, Patience spotted the wooden cot where her clothing had been laid out. She had almost certainly been undressed so that she could be re-dressed in something befitting a funeral. She sighed and began the lengthy process of dressing herself. She already had the underpants, stockings, and chemise. Atop those, she placed her petticoat. Without assistance, the bodice and skirt that came next were a challenge. She fiddled with the strings for a good ten minutes before deciding that the crooked, half-tied result was good enough. After all, that layer was about to be covered by her gown, which itself would be covered by her apron. When she was sufficiently covered and sweating hard from the layers, she picked up the lantern. She held it low and looked for any sign of life in the undertaker. There was none, so she moved along.

The next room was filled with metal instruments, chemical concoctions, and partially built coffins. Patience hurried through it, holding no desire to spend a second more in there than was necessary. What she would do when she got to the exit, she had no idea. She didn't have much time to come up with an idea, either. Puritan buildings weren't large. The undertaker had exactly three rooms and she had already explored two of them. The third was a foyer and shouldn't have counted as a room at all.

Patience approached the door with trepidation, but when she opened it, she found that Salem was basically a ghost town. At seven o'clock, it was late enough that everyone had retired for the evening. Unable to go home or to anyone else's home without causing a scene, Patience did the one thing she knew to do: she headed for the trees.

6 / TIME AND A BOTTLE

Sometimes, Agent Brooks ranted in Spanish. It wasn't the best Spanish, as he'd learned it from his very white father and not from his very dead mother, but it felt right. It also allowed him to express his ever-growing frustration with his partner without hurting his feelings—assuming Smith had any.

"*No tienes dos dedos de frente*," Brooks said. "*¡Manda huevos!*"

"I don't have two fingers?" Smith wondered. "Send eggs?"

Brooks was not amused.

The ferry ride back to Manhattan continued in uncomfortable silence. It wasn't so much the fact that Smith had drugged Brooks, dragged him unconscious to the backseat of a cab and then left him there as it was the fact that Smith had drugged Brooks, dragged him unconscious to the backseat of a cab, left him there and *didn't pay the driver*. That was the cherry atop this particular shit sundae.

The ferry was decidedly more crowded going toward Manhattan than it had been leaving it, probably because it was now moving away from Staten Island. The elderly coughed, the young spoke in expletives, and the children squawked in that peculiar way they do when it almost sounds like words but none of it makes any sense.

"I'mma wanna giball" said one child, who stared at Smith.

"What the fuck do you want?" Smith replied.

Brooks tilted his head in silence, then reached under his partner's seat to retrieve a small purple ball. He handed it to the child.

"Tanku, misteel," it responded, then pranced away.

"*What the fuck do you want?*" Brooks imitated, attempting to shame his partner. It didn't work.

Smith rolled his eyes. "He can't even figure out how to say

'ball.' He's not gonna retain 'fuck.'"

"What if that were *our* kid?"

Smith snorted. "Barkin' up the wrong tree, Brooksy." That was never going to happen.

Brooks put himself back on topic. "That's not the point. Why are you being so hostile?"

"Have you ever known me not to be?" Smith asked.

Brooks actually had, on occasion. "You know what I—"

In the background, the child repeatedly chirped "fuck" at its hapless mother. She took the ball, sauntered outside, and threw it into the bay as punishment. The child began to wail. At that point, everyone aboard became agitated in the way that only a screaming child can compel. They were especially on edge having just spent time on Staten Island.

"Shut that kid up!" one man shouted.

"Throw him overboard," added another.

The mother defended herself. "He's a kid, assholes."

"Fuck," the child giggled.

Brooks ignored the commotion, as he ignored most of the commotion Smith caused, and continued discussing the numerous matters at hand. While there had never been a time when Smith was agreeable, there had been a time when he was less aggressive—a time when he wouldn't have bitched at their boss, drugged his partner, or cursed at a child. It seemed to Brooks that there had been a change during the past year, and because berating Smith would get him no closer to understanding the reason, he moved to a different line of interrogation.

"Why do you even have Valium on you?" he asked.

"Not here," Smith said, certain that while he was white trash, he wasn't white trash enough to fight about drug use on public transportation.

"Eddie." Brooks paused. "Are you on drugs again?"

Smith laughed because his partner sounded just like an anti-drug PSA. "No. They can piss test us whenever they want. You know that."

"Then—"

"Old prescription I had lying around," Smith said.

"Bottle dated last month," Brooks corrected. "Hi. I'm a detective."

Smith loathed it when Brooks was concerned. The words *if he knew* kept repeating in his mind, but he couldn't share the happy little secret he'd been keeping for ten years. That would make matters definitively worse. There was, however, one truth he could share. Maybe it would be enough.

"I've been drinking a lot," he said. It wasn't the problem, but pretending it was might keep Brooks off his trail. The drunk detective stereotype was an asset, and he used it as such. Before the other man could get a word in, Smith raised a silencing finger and continued. "I know it's a problem. I'm on it. They gave me the Valium to help with withdrawal. Yes, the Reticent know." He exhaled. "You satisfied?"

Brooks was not. He shook his head. "I just want to know why." Smith's past substance abuses tended to coincide with stressors, and there weren't any. "Aside from work being a dud, things have been pretty great."

No they fucking have not, thought Smith. He couldn't explain himself further without lying, and he was a horrible liar, so he shut his partner down. "Because I have an insatiable desire to ruin my life, okay?"

He saw Brooks trying to look him in the eyes and turned his head away.

"Eddie—"

Smith didn't turn back.

They spent the rest of the ride in silence, or what would have been silence had there not been a child constantly shouting, "Fuck fuck fuck!"

⁎⁎

Back at Reticent headquarters, things went only slightly better than they had on the ferry ride. No sooner than Agents Brooks and Smith silently hung their coats, Agent Nguyen ushered them to the sixteenth subfloor conference room.

There were conference rooms, and then there was *the* conference room. This was *the* conference room, with plush leather office chairs meant only for the most important derrieres, and an on-staff bartender. It took the bulldozing of several acres of rainforest to make the peltogyne conference table, and close inspection revealed little bits of the endangered dart frogs that had been caught up in the process. The room was filled with important suits, and somewhere between entering the room and taking a seat at the back of it, Smith wished he could utilize the bartender. Seemingly reading that thought, Brooks put a hand on his partner's knee and offered a look of consolation. Smith found that partly sweet but mostly annoying; he did not require supervision.

His gaze abruptly left his partner when Agatha Werewith entered the room. The two had only interacted with the Reticent's aged leader once before at an awards ceremony, but they knew that her presence meant two things: one, that the smell of Estée Lauder White Linen would soon fill the room and nauseate everyone, and two, that their situation was serious, possibly to the point of being dire.* Werewith sat at the head of the table and the door was closed behind her. No latecomer would dare interrupt.

"Gentlemen," she said, ignoring that there were non-men in the room. "We have a problem."

Some heads nodded. Who they were didn't matter; they would all be replaced within months. No one at the agency's highest levels lasted very long.

---

* Actual Reticent incident severity rankings, in order: Unimportant, Concerning, Consequential, Serious, Dire, Überdire. The founders were dramatic, and had a poor grasp of German.

Werewith stared in the direction of the two agents who'd forced her to cancel a lunch date. "Code Fourteen. Agent Smith, would you care to explain?"

Smith suppressed the urge to answer "fuck no" and offered, in a disgustingly professional tone, "Agent Brooks and I were investigating the disappearance of Dr. Hudson Marrow, an old physics professor out of Staten Island. In his apartment, we found plans for a time machine, what looked to be that time machine, and a room full of historic artifacts which we believe to be authentic."

"Agent Brooks?" she asked.

"I concur with that assessment," Brooks said. He slid the blueprint across the table and Werewith glanced at it.

"I see." She addressed the entire room. "Gentlemen, if no one objects, I would like to direct Agents Brooks and Smith to attempt to use this time machine."

No one objected, which caused Smith to vehemently object. He stood and slammed his hands down on the frog-filled table. "I'm willing to use this thing, but is nobody here going to raise an issue?" In fact, he was very uncomfortable with the direction and hoped someone would join him in protest. A few suits made coughing sounds, but nobody did. He continued, "Isn't the whole reason Code Fourteen is *Code Fourteen* that it's a potentially *apocalyptic* scenario? For fuc— goodness sake, Code Thirteen is a supervolcano and Code Fifteen is a biblical fight between angels and demons."

"We've weighed the risks," Werewith said.

"In a little over an hour?" Smith asked. "Yeah, you've really given it some thought."

Brooks grimaced at his partner's outburst.

Werewith simply dismissed it. "You may have been under the mistaken impression that the purpose of this meeting was to *discuss* the situation with you. It was not. It was *to inform you of your next duty.*"

Smith bit his lip to keep himself from saying something

stupidly furious or furiously stupid, and the agents were promptly dismissed.

Afterward, Brooks noticed a change in his partner's demeanor. Smith stopped making eye contact altogether, and kept doing this thing where he pulled at his knuckles as though he were cracking them, but they never cracked. Even the Steve Buscemi situation hadn't made Smith nervous. It rubbed off on Brooks and soon there were two very anxious men heading back to Staten Island.

"You have any more Valium?" Brooks asked.

He was only half kidding.

7 / TIME TOURISTS

Lemon dabbed a spot of vomit off her cheek with a towel. It was a Batman beach towel, which she would have normally found odd coming from the President of an entire satellite. All things considered, though, it wasn't the strangest part of her day.

"Mr. President?" she asked.

"Call me Stan," said the President.

Lemon gulped. "Is this a time machine?"

Stan nodded.

The pod hadn't quite come to a stop, but it had slowed and was currently suspended somewhere in time and space. All that had ever been and all that ever would be surrounded them, and it looked like chocolate pudding. The machine was still spinning in the pudding, but very slowly as the group neared their destination, and Lemon's nausea had subsided. She no longer felt attached to the wall.

"Why did you bring me with you?" she asked.

"I don't function well without your brother, and he insisted," Stan said.

"Why didn't we know time machines exist?" she asked.

"This is the only one. I promised a friend I'd never use it again, but things were looking pretty bad back on Luna, and I didn't see any other options."

"What's going on with Luna?" Lemon asked. "Terrorists again?"

While it was common for hipsters to squabble over which fair trade standard was the fairest, which musician had sold out the hardest or which beard oil left beards the softest, they were at heart a peaceful people. Violence had come to the moon only when the government announced it would no longer allow home brewing because there were too many irradiated beverages being passed around. That had led to the frequent bombing of government-run beer distribution centers, though usually not during business hours. They were peaceful bombings.

"Relax," Stan said, like a man going through the motions.

"Relax?" Lemon's eyes widened. "All of my friends are back there!"

"You don't have any friends," Tangelo teased. Having already been advised of the President's plan, he was not worried.

Having already heard that line hundreds of times, Lemon was not amused. She crossed her arms, then uncrossed them to brace herself against the diner booth. Still spinning.

"If everything goes according to plan," Stan said, "they'll never know you were gone. We'll return to the exact moment we left, and Luna will be fine."

"So... is it terrorism?" she asked again.

"Hardly. There's a rift in time and space that needs to be repaired. I already know who can succeed at fixing it. We just have to find him."

"So where are we looking?" Lemon asked.

"When," Tangelo corrected.

"1692," Stan replied.

Lemon misheard that as 1962, and became excited at the prospect of meeting ? and the Mysterians at the band's founding. She should have tempered her expectations.

8 / JIM CROCE DIDN T KNOW SHIT

Smith looked into Brooks's eyes. "Any last words?"

"We're not even there yet," Brooks answered, giggling.

Smith hadn't given his partner the Valium he'd requested, but Brooks had done himself the courtesy of downing four shots of gin before he reboarded the Staten Island Ferry. This time, there would be no panic attack. There would be no horrific memories of wraiths and blood and death. There would be no fuck mode. The only thing out of the ordinary would be Brooks loosening up and enjoying himself. Also the time machine.

"This is bad," Brooks slurred. "This is really, really bad."

"The time machine? Yeah. It's pretty bad."

Brooks giggled again. "No, not that. I shouldn't be drinking. It's not right with your... uh... condition."

"You knock yourself out," Smith said. "Literally, if you want." He would never discourage anyone else from drinking when he had a hard enough time discouraging himself. Life, in his own eloquent words, sucked, so whatever it took to help people cope was fine by him. Besides, Brooks had always shown himself to be a pleasant drunk.

"I miss my sister," Brooks said unpleasantly.

"Uh, I'm sorry?" Smith wasn't sure how to handle this. Brooks didn't talk about his family, ever. Maybe with his therapist, but never with him. The one time he tried to— when they were on vacation in Maine, of all places—the conversation had ended their trip prematurely.

"It's fine. You didn't do it. I just... miss my family." Brooks's drunk mind decided to turn the topic on his partner. In addition to a pleasant drunk, he was a chatty one. "Do you?"

"I never met your family," Smith said. "I don't know—"

"No, I mean... do you ever miss *your* family?"

Smith snorted. "Uh, no."

"Not at all?" Brooks wondered.

That depended on which family Brooks was referring to. Smith's biological parents—and they were nothing more— died in a meth lab explosion when he was seven. After a few years of being bounced between twenty-six different families in the Indiana foster system, he had been adopted by Lucy and Charles O'Grady. The O'Gradys were an older couple who could no longer create the third child they had always wanted. They gave Smith everything he'd ever needed from a family, and he'd repaid them by barely making his way through high school on a bender, refusing to change his last name, and corrupting their biological children. Brooks knew all of this, and Smith was agitated that he would bring it up.

"What difference does it make?" Smith asked. "Even if I wanted to—*and I don't*—I can't see them again."

"*Pfft*. At least your family is still alive. You could see them if you really wanted to..."

"I slept with my stepsister," Smith said. "You don't... I mean... fuck."

"Hey, banging is a two way street," Brooks slurred, a little too loudly. Several other passengers gave him a concerned look. "They don't seem to have a problem with *her*."

"Yeah, well... they have a problem with me," Smith said.

In truth, the O'Gradys called their estranged son at least once a month, hoping that someday he would return the call. Smith was the only thing keeping himself isolated, out of some combination of self-loathing, disappointment, and fear. He had enough of all three to keep him away for decades, easily.

The ferry docked once more, and the men made their way to Hudson's apartment. To both agents' chagrin, it was empty once more. If they had encountered Hudson Marrow, they would have had to interrogate him, and any number of pressing matters could have arisen—matters that would mean a delay in using the mysterious time machine they knew nothing about.

With no scapegoat, the detectives made their way toward the bedroom. Brooks had the blueprint in hand, but it swiftly left his hand when he tripped over the door threshold. Smith reached out but couldn't get a handle on his drunken partner. Brooks landed half on the bed, half off, with his ass in the air. He began cackling like a movie villain who had simultaneously enacted his evil plan and realized he was about to be defeated.

"That's not even funny," Smith said.

Brooks spoke between laughs. "It's pretty funny." He lurched forward and allowed himself to fall completely onto the bed. Lying on his stomach, he whined into a quilt. "Help. I've fallen and I can't get up."

"Too bad we didn't get you a Life Alert when we had the chance," Smith said.

"Help me, Agent Smith!" Brooks's giggles continued.

"Okay, you're *very* drunk." Smith dropped down next to his tipsy partner. "You know we have a job to do."

Normally, those words would have whipped Brooks right into shape. As it was, they simply made him giggle some more and make jerking motions with his hand. "Yeah we do."

Smith smiled. "I wish you were drunk more often."

Brooks rolled onto his side and faced his partner. "What's that s'posed to mean?"

"It means I like you better without the stick up your ass."

Brooks snorted. "That's not true."

Smith snickered, then put a hand to his partner's cheek. "Really. You think there's something wrong with me, and... you're right. I'm all kinds of fucked. But there's something wrong with you too." He tried to articulate what was bothering him. "We didn't get where we are by worrying about retirement accounts and starting families."

"There's only so much time, " Brooks said. "I just want to make sure I use it right."

"What do you mean?" Smith asked. The phrasing seemed like that of someone who knew the same thing he did.

But Brooks didn't answer. Instead he kissed his partner in a successful bid to distract him. Smith rolled on top of him and started kissing him harder.

Brooks pulled back. "The time machine could kill us."

"Yeah, it could," Smith said. In fact, he had a strong feeling that 'could' would be better expressed as 'will.' He decided to make their last moments together count.

9 / PATIENCE WEARING THIN

Patience had nobody to talk to, and even if she did there was no way she would tell them about her condition. After thinking about it for a long time, she had come to the conclusion that she was cursed. Whether a witch or God had done it didn't matter. For her, there was simply no other explanation for how she went from dead to shocking the Salem undertaker dead.

She kicked a rock as she walked the same path she had when she found the bedeviled letter. It wasn't that she would miss Salem. It was a terrible town filled with terrible and terrified people. It was that she could think of nowhere else to go. She had no money and the automobile hadn't been invented yet. Her best chance, she reasoned, was to keep walking until she found a town far enough away that it hadn't heard rumors of the undead girl. There she could pretend to be an orphan and maybe—maybe—find someone kindly enough to take her in. It was rumored that distant towns weren't quite as chaotic as Salem.

While she couldn't die, Patience could become sore and tired, so she stopped for a moment to sit on a log. Before she could realize that sitting on a fallen tree isn't relaxing at all, she was knocked backwards off it. Her lantern too tumbled to the ground, extinguishing itself and leaving her in total darkness. That is, until a twenty foot radius nearby became flooded with green light. Patience peeked out from behind the log and had no idea what she was looking at. She had never seen a cartoon spaceship, so she had no point of reference to describe it. She dropped back behind the log and, because the whirring sound the machine made was horrible, plugged her ears with her fingers.

That lasted all of two seconds before the sounds of nature

prevailed once more.

That lasted all of three seconds before the sound of Agent Smith gagging triumphed over all. The inside of the time machine contained a dim lighting fixture, and Smith stumbled away from its gleam so he could puke in private. He braced an arm against a tree and let loose.

"Fuck this," he groaned amidst his retching. Time travel felt like someone had been pinching him to death from the inside out while forcing him to listen to bluegrass.

Brooks found it to be only mildly uncomfortable.

"We made it," he announced to no one in particular as Smith fell to his knees, gagging.

Patience peeked over the log once more to see the source of the voices. They appeared to be men, but of course demons were supposed to feign humanity in order to deceive. On the other hand, these two were wearing neither hats nor ruffs and their faces were beardless. Would demons not take care to blend in seamlessly? Plus, the standing man was tall and handsome, and his movement was gentle as he stepped away from the container he arrived in. Patience found herself ashamed of her thoughts.

A sobering Brooks saw the young woman peering at him. "There's a girl at three o'clock."

Patience didn't know what time it was, but as the sun was slowly rising in the distance, she was certain that it had to be past three.

Smith attempted to pick himself up off the ground. "Great. Now we can create a time paradox and destroy the universe." He paused, realizing the significance of that thought. "Can we? Can we do that?" He gagged and dropped back to his knees.

"I don't know," Brooks admitted. He grabbed his partner's hand and helped him up. Something about the way he did it gave Patience the impression that the handsome man would not be as interested in her as she was in him.

"Miss," Brooks said, looking directly at her.

She ducked.

"We've already seen you," Brooks said, prompting her shy emergence.

Smith wiped his mouth with the sleeve of his jacket. "We have to take her back."

Brooks agreed. "I know."

It was a matter of procedure. The Reticent didn't really know how to handle time travel, but the guidelines for it were clear: nobody in the past was permitted to see a member of the organization from the future. If they did, they were to be detained.

Patience approached slowly, keeping her head down. Her appearance betrayed her time period, even if one agent wasn't sure of the proper nomenclature.

"Pilgrim," Smith said.

"Puritan," Brooks corrected. When he had inputted their destination into the machine, he had typed 1692 in hopes of landing January 6, 1992. On that date, his grandparents had taken him and Tasha to the Detroit International Auto Show, so he knew there was no chance he would encounter his past self. He realized he'd actually inputted a year that was too late for pilgrims. Brooks directed the conversation to Patience. "Could you tell me where we are?"

"A short walk from Salem, sirs," she said, head still down.

"Salem, Massachusetts?" Brooks wondered.

"Yes, sir."

Brooks turned to Smith. "That answers the question of whether this thing can travel through space as well as time." They were no longer on Staten Island, but they may have found the one place in time and space that was worse. He turned back to the girl. "Have you seen any other people like us recently?"

"People like you?" she questioned.

"Sorry. My name is Arturo Brooks. This is Edward Smith.

You are?"

"Patience Cloyce," she said with a curtsy.

"Patience, we're looking for people who dress or look like us. People who don't look like pilgrims."

"Puritans," Smith corrected with a grin.

Brooks scowled. "Now you've got me doing it."

"No," she answered, "but I did find a letter on strange, bright paper."

"Bright paper?" Brooks asked.

The agents eyed each other. That was no good. If Hudson had left a letter, it could change the course of history. At least they thought. They weren't really experts in the field of time travel (after all, who was?), so their intent was to play it safe. Jump in, jump back, tell the Reticent it worked, and call it a day. 'Bring a Puritan girl back' made their to-do list a little more complicated. 'Go into the population center and look for a letter' would make it downright dangerous.

"Do you have the letter?" Smith asked.

"No," Patience said. "The elders burned it."

"Oh." That was good news. If the letter was gone, it probably couldn't cause much trouble. But the statement left Brooks wondering. "Why did they burn it?"

She relayed her story—just the parts about the letter, conveniently leaving out the immortality bit—and the agents were relieved that all the paranoia over witches had left the townspeople unable to conceive of other explanations for a time-displaced suicide note. They hadn't considered a single possibility other than witches, which was perfect. No muss, no fuss. Now it was time for the hard part: forcing the girl to return to the future with them.

"This is going to be difficult to believe," Brooks said, "but we're from the future—from the year 2014. Now that you've seen us, we need to take you back there."

"As you wish," she answered. If this was the fate God wished her to have, it was the fate she would embrace. What they said didn't have to make sense. Fate was all there was to it.

"Wait, really?" Smith said.

"Yes, sir. I'll go."

It was surprisingly easy. Brooks considered that if they were worse people, they could have gotten the naïve fifteen year old to do almost anything. He knew that the future was full of worse people, and he mentally vowed to make sure nothing bad happened to Patience. That is, nothing worse than being ripped from her home and family and taken to a time when she would understand almost nothing. Brooks wasn't sure she fully understood that part, so he took a moment to explain.

"Do you understand that you'll never see your family again?" he asked.

Patience nodded. "Yes, that's fine."

"That's *fine*?" Smith asked.

"Yes, sir. They hanged me for witchcraft."

That part intrigued Smith. Had he been drinking at the time, he would have done a spit take.

"You survived?" he asked.

"Yes, sir."

Brooks continued his original speech. There was no way Patience would truly understand until she arrived in 2014, but he had to try. "The future is going to be wildly different from what you're used to and it's going to be really, really scary to you. Do you understand that?"

"Yes, sir," she said, certain that God would never give her more than she could handle.

Brooks stepped up into the time machine, took Patience's hand, and helped her up into the diner booth. She shimmied against the seat's padding; it was the softest thing she'd ever felt. Sinfully luxurious.

Smith braced himself against the threshold. "How about I just stay here," he said, dreading another round of time travel. "I could fit in with pilgrims."

Brooks shook his head, and Smith silently took a seat across from Brooks and Patience. He spread his arms wide, bracing himself for takeoff. Brooks inputted their return time using the worn keypad—still unsure how the damn thing moved through space. Within seconds, they were spinning through the puddingy universe.

Patience took to time travel surprisingly well—so well that Smith was annoyed. He couldn't possibly be the only person who felt sick from being thrashed around the space-time continuum. He just couldn't. He looked across the booth, saw that his fellow travelers were unfazed, and scowled.

When the machine came to a loud, bright halt back at Hudson's apartment, Brooks failed at his vow to look out for Patience almost immediately. He ushered her from the time machine into Hudson's bedroom, where a handful of Reticent agents greeted them, guns pointed.

"Nice to see you too," Smith said, bracing himself against Hudson's dresser and suppressing the urge to vomit. He had to prove he was stronger than a fifteen-year-old pilgrim.

"What's going on?" Brooks asked.

One nameless agent answered. "We have orders to take the girl back to headquarters."

Patience's eyes grew wide as she noted the very different, very dangerous guns pointed her way. Were those the scary things in the future that Mr. Brooks told her about? Were all young girls abducted and taken somewhere? What was the strange small box next to the bed that displayed square numbers in an offputtingly orange shade? Why did the nice men seem so concerned? Should she be concerned? She decided that she should probably be concerned, and hid herself behind the nice men.

"How did you even know we were bringing her back?" Smith asked. He had a well-developed sense of when shady shit was about to go down, and that sense was tingling.

"I don't ask questions," the grunt said. "Just hand her over."

Patience looked at her captors/rescuers pleadingly. Her face seemed to say "please don't let them take me." She actually said nothing, as it wasn't her place to interrupt a group of men. The look made Brooks and Smith want to resist their orders, but they were in no position to do so. The most skilled secret agent in the world wouldn't have been able to escape that bedroom without being riddled with holes. And, all facts being faced, Brooks and Smith were not the most skilled agents in the world. The Goblin King situation had been 70-80% luck. They were helpless here.

Soon Patience was escorted out of the room as the two agents looked on. She glanced back at them, eyes still pleading.

"I'm sorry," Brooks said.

Smith noticed that his partner was nearly in tears over a girl they had known for about fifteen minutes, and something dawned on him.

This must be how it starts, he thought.

10 / MAN OUT OF TIME

There was never really silence in their neighborhood, but Brooks and Smith were as close to it as possible. The men hadn't said a word to each other in nearly an hour, and only the sound of low-pressure running water filled their kitchen. That was about to change.

"Mother of fuck," Smith said.

"Hmm?"

Brooks was busy washing dishes. He wasn't sure how they were dirtied in the first place, but he resented the fact that their Decatur Street brownstone had no dishwasher. It was 2014. There was no excuse for this. No excuse other than their near poverty. Paranormal investigation wasn't a lucrative profession, and if it hadn't been for Norman Brooks's generous life insurance policy, they would have been living in a rat-infested studio marketed as "artsy" or "BoHo." In any case, the sound of water rushing into the sink drowned out his partner's voice.

"I said MOTHER OF FUCK," Smith repeated, raising his voice.

Brooks turned the faucet off. "What?"

"They knew we were going to come back with some pilgrim girl," said Smith.

"Puritan," Brooks corrected. He dried his hands and took a seat at their table.

"Who gives a shit?" Smith paced the kitchen. "How did they know we were going to bring Patience back?"

Brooks thought about it. "Well... if it always happened, maybe they have records of us appearing in Salem."

Smith seated himself next to his partner. "Nobody else saw us. It doesn't make sense. And then they just took a teenager, and for what?"

"Maybe she's evil. Maybe there's something in Prophecies Division we don't know about."

Smith raised his brow. "She seem evil to you?"

Brooks remembered the wide eyes begging him to keep their owner safe. "No."

"Didn't think so," Smith said.

"You know who we work for," Brooks said. The Reticent were shadier than some amateur pencil work, but Brooks couldn't use that to justify what had happened on Staten Island. "Still... kidnapping kids..."

"That's what I'm saying," Smith said. "We're supposed to fight monsters, not little girls. It's screwy."

"Yeah." There was a moment of silence. "You know what else is screwy—"

"Oh, I swear on Carl Sagan's ashes..." Smith went from irritable to downright furious in a flash. "I told you I'm sorry. I did what I had to do to get you onto Staten Island."

"Not that. I'm talking about the drinking. You're not fine. The Reticent don't know. I just cleaned six whiskey glasses and I haven't had a drink here in a week."

"Those were for water," Smith lied. It was unconvincing.

"I don't know why you even try to lie," Brooks said. "You're getting worse and worse."

"'Worse and worse' implies I was ever good." Smith scoffed. "Don't get involved with shit and be surprised when it stinks."

"You're not—" Smith's opinion of himself killed Brooks, but there was no point in arguing. "Do you remember when we first met?"

Smith rolled his eyes. "No. It was just your run-of-the-mill monster attack. I'd completely forgotten."

"You were an *asshole*, Eddie. Seriously. Then I got to know you and you weren't. Now you are again, and I want to know why."

Smith rolled his eyes again. "I don't know what you're

talking about." For a brief moment, he considered telling his partner what was bothering him. He decided against it, the words *he can never know* echoing in his mind.

Brooks rubbed at his temples. "If you won't talk to me, we can't do this anymore."

"What does that mean?" Smith asked.

"It means... we can't be together."

Smith's eyes became heavy. "I wish I could tell you, but I can't."

"What do you mean, *can't?*" asked Brooks.

"I mean..." Smith stared directly into his partner's eyes. "I *literally* cannot tell you what's bothering me."

Brooks picked up on that. "Does this have something to do with the time machine?"

"Couldn't tell you," Smith said, staring and forcing his eyes to indicate "yes" as hard as he could.

"Have you time traveled before?" At this point, Brooks couldn't help but gesticulate wildly. Time travel was huge enough without the revelation that his partner had done it before. If he had, it was... well, huger. More huge? Brooks pondered the superlative for a brief moment.

"Couldn't tell you," Smith repeated deliberately.

That answer combined with the single manly tear running down Smith's cheek confirmed for Brooks that the answer was yes. But it didn't tell him everything he needed to know.

"Is something going to go wrong? With you? With me? With us?" He knew he wouldn't get an answer, but he couldn't contain the words.

Smith, meanwhile, came close to a total breakdown. He pictured the inevitable. For good measure, he pictured it again. "I can't tell you, okay? Code Fourteen. Code. Four-teen. Shit." The four words kept repeating in his mind: *he can never know.*

Before Smith could utter any further expletives, the whirring sound returned. The green light soon joined it, filling their small kitchen. Then there was a time machine blocking the path from kitchen to living area. Out stepped Hudson Marrow, if the picture at his apartment was anything to go by. He looked exactly like that man, but older and even fatter. His hair was starting to gray and there were slight wrinkles scattered about his face. He glanced around the room, noted that only the two agents were present, and approached them as they each wiped tears from their eyes. Smith cleared his throat.

"Agents Brooks and Smith?" the time traveler asked.

The men nodded to affirm that those were indeed their names.

"Have you met me yet?" Hudson asked.

"No?" Brooks said, unsure whether to phrase his answer in the form of another question.

"I'm sorry to do this to you, but I need your help."

11 / DON'T CALL IT A FLASHBACK

In 2004, Edward Smith insisted on being called by his full first name. In fact, the last person who called him "Eddie" ended up needing three stitches, a fact that Smith was neither proud nor ashamed of. He was stuck in traffic, heading for the Lincoln Tunnel on his way back from a bust vampire situation in Trenton, New Jersey. The car the Reticent had loaned him was a piece of crap—a Pontiac Aztek with 100,000 miles on it. How anyone had gotten an Aztek up to 100,000 miles, he wasn't sure.

The radio didn't work, so he was stuck with the one CD Agent Burroughs had left wedged in the seat: LL Cool J's *All World*. He considered the fact that LL Cool J had a greatest hits album and decided for about the thousandth time that the world was not just. His phone rang.

Erin Burroughs was on the line. "Is that LL?"

"Yeah, you left your CD in the car, if you can call it one."

"If I can call it a car, or if I can call it a CD?"

"Take your pick." Smith scowled at the line of parked cars in front of him. "What do you need?"

"I'm gonna knock you out. Mama said knock you out," LL said.

"I need you to get to Staten Island," Burroughs said.

"Seriously?"

"Seriously. There's a wraith attack at Willowbrook Park," Burroughs said. "They're sending everyone."

"Everyone but you?" Smith wondered.

"I'm gonna knock you out. Mama said knock you out," LL said.

"I'm on the ferry now, you ass."

Smith sighed. "Fine. I can be there in half an hour if I push it."

"Push it," Burroughs said.

Smith pulled an illegal maneuver and turned the Aztec around.

"I'm gonna knock you out. Mama said knock you out," LL said.

As soon as he arrived on the scene, Smith wished that LL Cool J had followed through on his threats. Willowbrook Park was a nightmare. Agents descended on the area from every direction. Pretending they were police officers or FBI agents so they could fend off actual officers and FBI agents was going to be a nightmare. Pretending the wraiths were Russians hopped up on a new drug called krokodil was going to be a bigger nightmare. Their entire operation was becoming a nightmare now that seemingly everyone had a cell phone. And the phones were becoming "smart." Smith didn't know what that meant, but he didn't like it.

There were bodies everywhere, mostly human with the occasional wraith accent piece showing off its translucent skin and fangs. In the pantheon of Reticent monsters, wraiths were one of the rarest and most dreaded. Like vampires, wraiths possessed haunting yellow eyes and sharp fangs. Unlike vampires, they had a whole mouth full of them instead of two incisors. Like zombies, wraiths were resurrected corpses that consumed human flesh. Unlike zombies, they weren't slow and lumbering. They moved swiftly, like natural predators.

Smith met his partner near the park's carousel. "Jesus Christ," he said, noting what used to be a child smeared across the pavement and a felled ice cream cone smeared next to it. "How many were there?"

"We've killed two dozen," Burroughs said. "A few may have escaped, but we're getting it locked down."

He lit a cigarette. "They don't usually hunt in packs."

"No kidding. We're on perimeter duty. Come on." She knocked the cigarette out of his hand and gestured toward what was to be the perimeter in one sweeping motion.

As they headed across the field, Smith made a fourth attempt at hitting on his partner. "So, about the other night..."

"About you hitting on me in the cafeteria?"

"Yeah, that. I never got to finish."

"Rules are rules, Eddie."

He bit his lip. "*Edward*. And rules were made to be broken."

"Are you seriously hitting on me at the worst crime scene we've ever seen?" There were many lows, but this one was absolute zero.

Smith shrugged. Tall and brunette, Burroughs was just his type, and it wasn't like either of them really gave a shit about anyone from Staten Island. Before he could say something to that effect, a guttural scream interrupted from the other side of the carousel.

A young man sat atop the carousel looking down at three wraiths: two eating a young woman and another tearing an old man to pieces. Smith and Burroughs ran toward the scene as quickly as they could. As they approached, the man leapt from the roof into the pack.

"What the hell is he doing?" Smith asked, drawing his gun. "He's going to get himself killed."

One of the wraiths grabbed the beautiful, stupid young man, sinking its claws into the side of his neck. Burroughs raised her gun and shot a silver bullet through its head. Smith shot the other two. The young man fell to the ground, trembling. His face and clothing were covered in his sister and father's blood. His neck was covered in his own. He kept muttering something softly to himself. When Smith neared, he could hear the words.

"*Dios te salve, Reina y Madre de misericordia, vida, dulzura y esperanza nuestra—*"

Internally, Smith rolled his eyes at the notion of prayer, but now wasn't the time, so he refrained. Instead, he took off his jacket and put it around the man. Since empathy wasn't really in his wheelhouse, he had what amounted to a script for situations like this. "Hey, you're gonna be fine." Smith paused. "Uh... *Tú vas... estar...*"

The young man looked at what remained of his sister, then to what remained of his father, then back at Smith. "No, I'm not," he said, shaking.

Smith was relieved at not having to botch the Spanish language any further. Reticent agents were trained to ask questions in situations like this. Questions, it was alleged, distracted trauma victims and kept them from being completely absorbed in their tragedies.

"What's your name?" he asked.

"A-Arturo Brooks," the man said.

"Edward Smith," the agent replied.

"What were those?" Brooks asked, eying the monsters Smith and Burroughs had just killed.

Smith stammered. "Uh... Russians. They have this drug called krokodil over there and..."

The man looked up, his brown eyes squinting at the detection of bullshit. "Don't lie to me."

"Wraiths," Smith said. "Like zombies, but smarter."

"Damn it, Eddie," Burroughs said. Her partner could never resist telling people about the supernatural. No fewer than six agents had been recruited as a result of Smith's blabbing.

"What? Dude just watched his girlfriend get her throat ripped out. He deserves to know why."

"My sister..." Brooks corrected.

"Sorry," Smith said, looking into the distance.

A pair of figures—silhouetted under a lamp—drew his attention. He started toward them.

"What are you doing? Burroughs asked.

"There's someone else in that field," he said. "Watch over 'Turo here. I'm gonna check this out."

Smith wandered out into the perimeter duty field. There, he found another man hunched over the body of a loved one. He repeated his script. "Hey, you're gonna be fine."

"Get the fuck out of here," the man said.

The man looked up and Smith found himself pale face-to-pale face with an older version of himself. A chill ran down his neck. There was no mistaking himself, and there were tears streaming down future-his face. Smith looked down at the ground and saw the corpse of the man he'd just met, equally older. His mind had trouble processing what was going on, and could only formulate three words: *Shit. Code Fourteen.* He tried to guess at the age of his older self and figured him to be about fifteen years older if he didn't age particularly poorly. He glanced from corpse to older self and back and his mind offered three more words: *Shit shit shit.*

"Don't say a word to Brooks," the older man cautioned between gasping breaths. "He can never know."

His future self's voice meant business, so Smith didn't ask questions. He backed away from the scene and forced his face to clear its expression. This was a Code Fourteen, and the consequences could be dire.

12 / TACHYON PARTICLES AND OTHER ODDITIES

In 2014, Hudson Marrow attempted to explain the dire consequences. Agents Brooks and Smith, however, couldn't follow his train of thought. Neither was an expert in theoretical physics. Neither was an expert in anything, really. Hudson picked up on this as the agents' eyes began to glaze over somewhere around his thirteenth use of the word 'quantum.'

"Let me put it another way," Hudson said, clearly annoyed. "Time travel can result in a number of paradoxes, and I believe one of them is happening right now."

"2014 right now?" Smith asked.

"Yes." Hudson explained that he was from the year 2090 and that, through a series of experiments neither agent could grasp, he found that the fabric of reality was beginning to tear. This was a cause for concern. "I tweaked the time machine to trace the source using some tachyon particles—"

"Like on *Star Trek*?" Smith asked. "Seriously?"

"That sounds made up," Brooks said.

The scientist shook his head with contempt. "I traced the source and it took me here."

"Okay, so why us? Why don't you go find Neil deGrasse Tyson or something?" Brooks asked.

Smith agreed. "I'm with him. This is stupid."

"Would you two..." Hudson buried his head in his hands, inhaled deeply, and then very slowly withdrew his hands. "I remember you both. You're the ones who found my time machine. It's the only one in 2014, so whatever is causing the disturbance... you should know about it."

"Okay. How about the giant pile of artifacts in your apartment?" Smith asked.

"Those were for research," Hudson said. "I always made sure to put everything back exactly where it came from."

Brooks sat at the table with his chin in his hand, silent.

His partner turned to him and offered a concerned look. "Brooksy?"

"I'm still stuck on the time travel. If you met us in 2014, and now future you is coming to meet us for the first time to stop a time paradox... obviously the universe doesn't end in 2014 so... what did you do the first time around?"

Smith stared at him. "I need a drink."

Brooks continued. "Did you ever stop to think that it's you?"

"Excuse me?" Hudson asked.

"It's gotta be you. 2090 you coming back to 2014 is the paradox," Brooks said.

"If that were the case, I wouldn't have detected the paradox in 2090 before I'd ever come back to 2014. When I lived through it, there was no paradox. I met you two breaking into my apartment and we parted ways."

"How about Patience?" Smith asked.

"Who?" Hudson asked.

"The pilgrim we brought back from the 1600s."

"YOU DID WHAT?" The physicist's shriek could be heard for miles. It was so loud that it muffled the sound of Brooks correcting his partner with the word 'Puritan.'

As Hudson paced back and forth, Brooks and Smith immediately picked up on the notion that they might have made a mistake.

"Those were our orders," Brooks said. "If someone sees us traveling through time, we have to bring them back to the present so they don't accidentally learn about the future and change history."

"Unless you changed history by bringing her here in the first place!" Hudson shouted.

Brooks scratched his head. "I didn't make the rules."

Hudson perked up at that remark.

"I need a drink," Smith repeated.

"Who made the rules?" Hudson asked.

"That's classified," Brooks said.

"The fabric of reality is tearing," Hudson said, "and you're worried about protecting your agency?"

"The Reticent," Smith said. "They took her. It's more a company than an agency. As far as anyone knows, we do medical research. The founder ran an apothecary, and—"

Brooks threw up his hands and interrupted. "Really? You can't resist telling *anyone*, can you?"

Smith shrugged. He'd ended up sleeping with each of the last six people he told about the Reticent, so it was working out pretty well for him so far. Not that he wanted to sleep with Hudson Marrow. Quite the opposite. There was something about him that filled Smith with disgust. Maybe it was the mystery stain on his collar. More likely, it was how similar he looked to Smith himself.

"We need to find the Puritan girl and put her back where she came from," Hudson said.

That would be easier said than done. They had no idea where Patience had been taken, who in the organization had ordered her capture, or who they could talk to about it.

"Then you're going to have to come over to HQ and tell them what you told us," Brooks said.

"Were you even listening?" Hudson asked. "If I interact with a bunch of people in this time period, that could make matters worse. I came to you two because you're my only option."

"I feel like you're leaving something out," Smith said.

"Yes. Obviously," Hudson answered.

Brooks sighed. He dialed Charlotte Nguyen and told her they needed to return Patience to the past. When pressed for more information, he danced around it. She was unimpressed and assured them that the Puritan was being handled with the utmost care. Those were her exact words: "utmost care."

"I really think you should take this seriously," Brooks said while the other men stared at him.

"I really think you should mind your own business," Nguyen retorted. "That's how you get from missing persons reports back into something more interesting: by doing what you're told. We hand out the assignments, not you."

When she hung up on him, Brooks made an uncharacteristic decision.

"We're gonna have to break in and get her," he said.

Smith was stunned. He stood and confronted his partner with his presence. "Pump your brakes there, chief. Do you understand what you're saying?"

Brooks nodded. "Of course I do."

Smith didn't think he did. "We will one hundred percent lose our jobs over this. Not only can you kiss your sweet, sweet retirement goodbye, but there's a good chance we end up hunted and killed."

"I know," Brooks said.

Smith knew they wouldn't be killed—not yet anyway—and it kept him from entering any true state of panic, but he still didn't like where his partner's mind was going on this. "It's probably not even possible. The security system..."

Reticent headquarters, housed in a building its founder constructed in the 1790s, was literally overflowing with security measures.* There were eye scanners, hellhounds, thumbprint readers, and a lie-detecting Dror. They could get in, sure. They worked there, after all. Getting to an area they weren't cleared to be in, though... that would be difficult. Clearances were very specific, as were the guidelines for what to do if someone tried to do something beyond their

---

* Literally. It had a moat. Granted, the moat was made of invisible pixie plasma, but it was a moat nonetheless.

clearance.

"We don't even know where she is," Smith pointed out.

"I know," Brooks said. "But if we broke the universe, I'd say we're obligated to fix it. Wouldn't you?"

Smith shrugged. It was a good reason to abduct Patience, but it still didn't seem like enough for Brooks to be breaking rules left and right. "That's it, though?"

"She's a kid," Brooks said.

Suddenly Smith understood.

"I'm not staying here," Hudson said. "I don't even know that coming here for half an hour wasn't a mistake."

Brooks nodded.

"Get the girl, get out, bring her to my apartment. Use the same machine that brought her here to take her back." With his instructions clear, he hopped back into his time machine and disappeared in a now-familiar burst of green light.

"I still need a drink," Smith said.

"No, you don't." Brooks entered serious mode and roped him in for an embrace. Smith rolled his eyes as Brooks continued. "You're gonna be fine. We're going to be fine. Whatever Code Fourteen happened or didn't happen, we'll be okay."

Smith chose to neither acknowledge nor respond to that naiveté.

"I wasn't serious about the drink," Smith said, pulling himself away slightly. "But if you're feeling touchy—" He lowered and raised his gaze a few times.

Brooks half-chucked and half-scoffed. "Seriously?"

Smith shrugged.

"After we save the world."

13 / A PLACE IN TIME

There was history, and then there was *history*. Lemon Jones had always wanted to travel to the early 2000s, maybe even to the 1980s. No, make that the late 1970s. She would have loved to have seen Bauhaus before they went mainstream. The 1690s, however, were a bit too far.

Stan grabbed a Clorox wipe from the compartment behind his seat and wiped her vomit off the diner booth that filled the time machine. He stepped outside, still holding the wipe, then realized he couldn't exactly throw it away in the woods outside Salem, Massachusetts. He stuffed it into the compartment it had come from, disgusted, knowing he'd have to clean that up later.

Tangelo stepped out after him, and Lemon followed. Stan put his hands out and gestured for them to stop. "This is Salem, Massachusetts, 1692," he said.

"So?" Tangelo said.

"So you're black," Stan said, rifling through a different compartment under his diner seat.

"Good point," Lemon said. "Can you at least tell us why we're here?"

"This is the earliest anyone alive came from," he said, grabbing the outfit he'd packed for the occasion.

That answer didn't make any sense, and Tangelo called the President on it. "You're saying someone from 1692 is alive in 2202?"

"Yes," Stan said.

"And we're here looking for him because—"

"*Her*," Stan corrected. "And because of that."

He pointed up at the sky and—as sure as President Sanford would die alone—there was a giant rift in time and space above the forests of Salem. Where there should have been sky, there was simply... nothing. Lemon took a few steps back, as if that would keep her safe from the empty void.

"You said we were looking for a him," Lemon said.

"Yes, indirectly. Whatever's happening in our time," Stan said, "it's connected to her. It's connected to this place. The man I'm looking for knows it."

"So what are we gonna do?" Tangelo asked.

"*You're* going to stay here and watch your sister," Stan said, pulling a cloak over his shoulders. He saw that Lemon was about to interrupt with something to the effect of "I don't need to be watched" and raised a finger to stop her. "*I'm* going to go into town and see what the good people of Salem have been up to."

He struggled to adjust the ruff he had squeezed around his neck. It was crooked and stupid looking, but it would have to do. He took a deep breath and began the walk toward town.

Lemon, meanwhile, took in the scenery. This was both her and her brother's first time traveling back in time, but more importantly for Lemon, it was her first time traveling to Earth. She'd read about it—certainly more than is healthy—and considered herself a history buff, but actually seeing it blew her mind.

"Are those—?" she asked.

"Trees?" Tangelo said. "Yes."

"Incredible," Lemon said.

14 / DAYS OF PASSED FUTURE

There was a cosmic tear in front of Reticent Headquarters; that was the best way of describing it. At street level, there was the old cobblestone building, deceptive as ever in its simplicity. At sky level lay that building's roof. In between, there was nothing. A large horizontal gash—about fifteen feet wide and three feet high—in which there was simply nothing. No purple glow or emerging dragons or anything that would happen in fiction. Just nothing. Nobody in New York seemed to notice; they were all too busy looking down at their phones or yelling at cab drivers. Brooks and Smith were the exceptions, and the tear reinforced their decision to betray their employer.

Brooks made one last attempt to reach Nguyen. He dialed her desk and asked if, perhaps, she had noticed the giant tear. She had, and she was not concerned, so the plan moved forward.

The two agents stared at the outside of the building for a moment, taking it in.

"This might be the last time we're here," Brooks said.

"Probably. I hope your passport's still good," Smith said.

They entered the building, bypassing all scanners as expected. From the lobby, the agents went their separate ways: Brooks to their office, and Smith to the twelfth subfloor. Each had a part to play in their hastily developed plan.

Gaining an audience with Agatha Werewith was not easy, but Smith made it happen. He could make a lot of things happen when he stopped drinking and swearing and actually tried to make things happen, which was rarely. In the hallways of the twelfth subfloor, just outside the cafeteria, he casually bumped into their CEO and knocked her cell phone out of her hand, taking care not to make any snide remarks about the fact that it was a BlackBerry.

"Oh, I'm so sorry," he said, bending down to retrieve the device.

"Agent Smith," she grumbled.

"I'm just out of it, you know? Ever since the Code Fourteen..." He took his time, fumbling with the phone and obscuring the screen from her view. "I think that machine made me sick."

Just when this was starting to take a bit too long, he handed her the phone. She eyed him suspiciously. "You look fine to me. Get back to work."

"Yes, ma'am," said Smith.

The plan was insane. Any plan concocted by Brooks and Smith in under twelve hours would have been insane, but this was at least better than Smith's "poison the food" plan. He returned to their office and held out his hand. Resting in his palm was the tiny SD card he'd yanked from Agatha Werewith's BlackBerry.

"Great," Brooks said, turning to his computer screen.

Smith leaned over his shoulder. "We need to work fast. If she tries to browse her pics or cat videos, it's all over."

"Why do you assume she has cat videos?" Brooks asked.

"Oh, she has cat videos."

"I'm on it," Brooks said, typing away.

It was a trick Agent Burroughs had taught them four years earlier. Every SD card comes equipped with a microcontroller; a few tweaks and inserting one into a phone could automatically execute some code. In this case, the code inserted into Werewith's phone would allow the agents access to their CEO's email. From there, finding what they were looking for was as tedious as explaining the logistics of SD card hacking.

"Search for 'Pilgrim,'" Smith said.

"For the last time..."

"I don't understand the difference," Smith admitted.

"I know you don't," Brooks said.

While both were early religious extremists, the word 'Pilgrim' refers to the very first, very small group of American settlers who came to Plymouth on the Mayflower. Puritans were wealthier and better educated, and possessed both greater numbers and a greater penchant for executing witches. Brooks was going to explain that, but Smith kept making stupid suggestions.

"Search for 'Patience.'"

Brooks sighed. "Do you think the email's going to be 'RE: Patience the Puritan We Brought Back in a Time Machine'?"

"And *I'm* the asshole," Smith remarked.

Brooks kept scrolling. "Sorry."

Smith really didn't care.

Agatha Werewith's inbox held thousands of messages, most of which were corporate red tape. Brooks clicked the Sent folder to narrow it down to the items Agatha had deemed worthy of reply.

RE: RE: RE: RE: Budget Cuts
RE: RE: RE: Budget Cuts
RE: RE: Cafeteria Service Provider
RE: RE: Budget Cuts
RE: Incident Report #235656
RE: Incident Report #235655
RE: Cafeteria Service Provider
RE: Budget Cuts
FWD: RE: FWD: PETITTION TO IMPEACH THE MUSTLIM PRESIDENT

"Probably an Incident Report..." Smith said.

"I don't know about you, but I'm interested in the Mustlim chain email." Brooks paused, perplexed. "Did you even file an Incident Report?"

"No," Smith said. "You?"

"No..." That was definitely not standard procedure.

"Just click until we find it then..."

The Incident Report they needed was #235653 (filed by Charlotte Nguyen), but before they found it, the agents learned a few interesting things about their employer. One: At least three of their coworkers were werewolves. Two: Agatha Werewith was having at least three affairs with some very young agents. Three: For budgetary reasons, Taco Tuesdays were going to be cancelled in favor of Stroganoff Tuesdays. It was a tragic moment for tacos and alliteration alike.

The Incident Report read as follows.

INCIDENT REPORT #235653

FILED: 14 September 2014, 0940

ASSIGNED AGENTS:
Brooks, Arturo
Goodwin, Casey
Nguyen, Charlotte
Smith, Edward

DETAILS:
At the request of Ms. Werewith, CEO and President of the Reticent, Agents Arturo Brooks and Edward Smith were directed to use the known time displacement device at 90 Bay Street Landing, Apartment 157, Staten Island, New York. They followed these directions and traveled to 1692. On their return, they brought with them a 15-year-old Puritan named Patience Cloyce. This happened as predicted in the archives. The girl, whom we know to be immortal, has been transferred to Agent Casey Goodwin in the Human Mutations department for research and experimentation.

"Do you know an Agent Goodwin?" Brooks asked.

"No. You?"

Brooks shook his head. "Human Mutations is on twenty-six, though."

Smith could see his partner's dread. The twenty-sixth sub-floor was the deepest of the building. If the agents were going to have to abduct someone from Reticent headquarters, of course she had to be in the place most unfavorable to their success.

"You sure we can't convince Charlotte?" Smith asked.

"Oh, I'm sure," Brooks said. "Werewith's orders. And according to the emails, she's got a bonus riding on this."

Smith exhaled. "Looks like we're breaking into twenty-six then..."

"If we don't make it..." Brooks grabbed his partner's hand and Smith remembered that this mission actually seemed dangerous to Brooks. "...you know."

"Yeah..." Smith hadn't mastered faux fear, even with ten years of practice. He reminded himself to keep making eye contact because eye contact was good for diffusing stress, according to the books. He awkwardly clasped Brooks's other hand and stared into his eyes long enough that it was disquieting.

Brooks felt no better about their gambit. He hovered the cursor over the Compose button for several seconds before proceeding with the plan.

15 / PATIENT

There were no advanced medical facilities in Salem, Massachusetts in 1692. Patience had grown up learning that God created all diseases as punishment for the Original Sin and all of its duplicate sins. If only God could create sickness, then only God could cure sickness and there wasn't much point to the field of medicine. For that reason, Patience was shocked by what she saw around her. The only machine she had ever seen was the time machine Brooks and Smith used to bring her to 2014. Now there were ventilators, computers, and the strangest thing of all: light bulbs, everywhere.

She had been disrobed and placed in a hospital gown of the finest material she'd ever felt. For a brief moment, she felt like royalty, and considered that she had died at the hanging and this was her heaven. That lasted until she realized that a) the gown had no back, and b) she was strapped to a cot and festooned with heart monitors.

Then came the experiments. A lethal injection, followed by a resurrection. Another lethal injection with the same result. Then another. Then another. The Reticent scientists were perplexed. They drowned her. She came back. They burned her. She came back. They decapitated her and that kept her dead for a while, but when they put the two pieces back together she healed and came back again.

At first, it was horrifying. With a few days' repetition, it became routine. She suffered like a pro (all Puritans did), but by the point of her dismembering, Patience had held her tongue as long as she could. The Devil was already in her, keeping her alive, so she figured talking back couldn't hurt her any further.

"How long are you going to keep me here?" she asked.

"Until we figure out how this works," Dr. Goodwin

answered. Like Patience, he was a short, thin ginger. Unlike Patience, he was in charge of her fate.

"How what works?" asked Patience.

"Your immortality," Goodwin said. "Is there anything you can tell me about how you got this way?"

"No, sir. I'm afraid I don't know."

"Then we're going to be here awhile."

"Could I have something to eat?" Patience asked. All the executions were making her hungry.

The doctors agreed, but when they brought a bagged grilled cheese sandwich from the cafeteria, they realized they hadn't yet starved her to death and declined to offer it. That, she felt, was rather rude.

As Dr. Goodwin took a bite of the grilled cheese sandwich, the two other doctors cut into her again. She winced at the pain of the scalpel splitting her skin, and tried to focus on anything else. In the next room, there was the creaking sound of a swinging door swinging open. She didn't know it was a swinging door; she just heard the FLAPFLAPFLAP as it kept swinging. FLAPFLAP.

Dr. Goodwin, still chewing, looked up from his sandwich to see two agents in lab coats.

"Jushaminute," he said.

FLAP. The door finished swinging and the doctor finished chewing. The men raised their ID cards.

"Agents Brooks, Smith," Brooks said. He glanced through the window into the room where Patience was being hacked into pieces. Luckily for her, she had passed out from shock some time ago. Regardless, it was a horrible thing to do to someone, and Brooks got quiet in the way he did when he could barely contain his anger. Smith could practically hear the Spanish expletives rattling through his partner's head.

"What can I do for you?" the doctor asked.

Smith began bullshitting. "There seems to have been a problem with Incident #235653. The lab work was sent to you when it was supposed to be sent to us. We're here to pick it up."

The doctor was confused. "What?"

"You should have received an email," Smith said with an air of high-level corporate disdain.

Goodwin unlocked his screen and opened his email. His eyes went as wide as they could when there was a message from Agatha Werewith herself. He fumbled over his words. "Uh, of course. Do you want the others to continue—"

"We'll need time to fully review the case. It would probably be best if you dismissed them for the time being," Smith said.

"Yes. Right away."

Dr. Goodwin nearly leapt into the operating area to clear the others. Such was the effect that Agatha Werewith had on sensible people. Brooks and Smith could see his cursory gestures through the glass. Whatever Goodwin said got Patience put back together in a hurry. The doctors glanced worriedly at the security camera as they hastily pushed her organs back into place. When everything seemed to be in order, they hurried out.

When the others were gone, Brooks and Smith stormed the room and began untying the girl. Her head shook back and forth for a moment as she came to. When she finally processed her surroundings, she sat straight up.

"You returned," she said, beaming. Then she pressed together a gash in her arm, which healed itself.

"Yeah, time paradox says it's your lucky day," Smith said.

She had no idea what he was talking about. Still, she was grateful to have her arms and legs free once more... and to have her arms and legs at all. She stood up, ready to flee the building in her hospital gown, forgetting that her backside was completely uncovered. Smith snickered.

At this point, Patience had been through enough that she would have been perfectly content to venture out in her luxurious new hospital gown. What was shame, really, compared to being dismembered? Brooks looked around the room for her dress, but frowned when he found nothing. He took off his lab coat, draped it over her shoulders, and watched as she tied the sleeves in front of her in an unusually tidy knot. The coat was so long that it dragged on the floor. Perfect for a Puritan girl.

"That'll do for now," he said. "Patience, we need you to stay quiet. Can you do that?" He already knew what the answer would be.

"Yes, sirs."

"We also need you to stop calling us sirs," Smith added.

Patience stayed quiet.

The agents looked around the room for something—anything—they could use to hide the teenager as they made their way topside. What they found was a room full of nothing. There was a cot, but rolling a patient into the employee elevator would have been even more suspicious than sauntering out with a half-dressed Puritan, and they didn't have their biometrics enrolled to use the medical elevator. So they fitted Patience with a pair of handcuffs and hoped for the best. There was a chance, however miniscule, that they could hop in the elevator and it wouldn't stop on another floor on their way to street level—that nobody would notice and they would scurry off, nobody wise to the heist they'd just completed until Agent Nguyen stepped into their office, saw Agatha Werewith's emails, and began shouting expletives.

While she would eventually step into their office, see the emails, and begin shouting expletives, the smooth escape was not meant to be. The moment they escorted Patience out of Human Mutations, they caught Dr. Goodwin's eye.

"Agents."

Brooks and Smith shared an unnerved look.

"I understand that #235653 is in your hands now, but you cannot remove the patient from this area," Goodwin said.

Smith concocted a story on the spot. "We're well aware of

Regulation 3.16.438, Doctor. The problem is... this facility is not appropriate for conducting the research we need to conduct. Do you know that none of your Erlenmeyer flasks have ground glass joints?"

The doctor snorted. "Come on. You know that's not a big deal."

"Really?" Smith asked, shaking his head in disgust. "I suppose you think the use of fabric restraints instead of leather or metal is 'not a big deal' either?"

"I..."

Brooks chimed in. "The fact of the matter is: this laboratory is unacceptable, and we're taking the patient up to Holding until that changes. If you check your email, you'll find we have authorization to do so."

"I... I understand."

Crestfallen, the doctor pressed the button for the elevator.

Only one person in Reticent history had truly experienced "forever." It was Alexis Larios, who fell victim to a demigod that showed her the entirety of human existence—past, present, and future—in the snap of a finger. She lost her mind, suffered a nonfatal aneurysm, then lost her mind again. After Larios, the two agents who came closest to experiencing "forever" were agents Brooks and Smith as they waited for this elevator. It didn't even do them the courtesy of displaying which floor it was currently on. For all they knew, it was only a floor away and the whole thing was packed with armed agents ready to murder them. It wasn't, but they didn't know that. Each time someone passed them in the hallway, they were convinced the jig was up. The closest call came in the form of an older gentleman who yelled at them from twenty feet away.

"Hey! You two!"

He rushed toward them and Smith moved his hand toward his gun a little too eagerly, but when the man reached the elevator, Brooks and Smith found that he was simply trying to sell chocolate bars to support his daughter's middle school AV club. Brooks bought three—one with almonds so he could be sure Smith wouldn't eat all of them—and the man went on his merry way.

After exactly six minutes and fourteen seconds, the elevator arrived, empty.

"That's convenient," Smith said.

"A little—"

"So help me, if you finish that with 'a little too convenient,' I will turn you in right here and now. Wash my hands of you. 'It was all his idea,' I'll say."

His attempt to speak like an 80s action hero thwarted, Brooks stepped into the elevator. "Guess we'll see," he said, crossing his arms.

The elevator started with the kind of jerk that old elevators start with, and they were off. The interior of the elevator came equipped with the floor counting technology the exterior lacked. It wasn't immediately clear whether that made matters better or worse.

25. DING.

24. DING.

23. DING.

22. DING.

21. DING.

20. DING.

19. DING.

18. DING.

At the eighteenth subfloor, a sense of relief overcame each of the agents. They were going to pull this off more smoothly than they had the assassination of Steve Buscemi. There wouldn't be any workplace kudos this time, but they could sleep well knowing they had saved the entire world from a paradox that they didn't understand but that was most definitely dire. Brooks smiled.

17. DING.

At the seventeenth subfloor, an intern entered the car. He was obviously an intern because he wore the face of a pizza delivery boy caught in headlights and the clothing of someone not being paid for his work. That intern was Jimmy Carhope, and he was so into following the rules that he actually wore his company badge above the waist—clipped to the pocket of his blue button-down straight from the softer side of Sears. Anyone who'd been with the Reticent longer than a few months just shoved their badge in their pants pocket.

Brooks and Smith stared at Jimmy in silence, each keeping a hand on Patience's shoulder to add to the illusion that they were escorting her. Jimmy, meanwhile, bit his lip and focused intently on a mental image of his New Employee Handbook. Section 1 was about proper workplace attire and conduct (i.e., how not to behave like Edward Smith). Section 2 outlined the 43 emergency codes for apocalyptic situations (e.g., Code Fourteen – Time Travel).* Section 3 was a very long, very boring series of policies and procedures, most of which were for filling out forms. Jimmy thought hard. There was something in there about patient transport. Something that didn't seem quite right. His face lit up.

16. DING.

Jimmy cleared his throat. "Sorry, I'm new here, but aren't patients supposed to be transported in the medical elevator so they don't pose a danger to other employees?"

"Yeah, it's down," Smith said.

15. DING.

Jimmy debated keeping quiet but decided against it. After all, if he encountered wrongdoing, he could be promoted to *paid* intern. "I'm sorry, but doesn't Section 3.17.4 state that if the medical elevator is down, patient transport is to be delayed until it's back up?"

"Yes it does. What's your name?" Brooks asked.

---

* See Appendix 1.

"Jimmy Carhope."

"Well, Jimmy, this is a special case."

14. DING.

Smith nodded. "We need to get this girl to Holding immediately. She poses a danger to all of the patients on Level 26."

13. DING.

Jimmy's eyes grew even wider. "But... Holding is on 18."

Brooks and Smith said nothing.

12. DING.

11. DING.

Jimmy glanced at the agents, then at the buttons lining the front of the elevator car. He was closest to them. They couldn't stop him from pressing Emergency Stop. On the other hand, they could murder him for doing so, and committing homicide was certainly something rogue agents were prone to doing, according to Section 4 of the New Employee Handbook: Reticent History and Significant Events. Of course, if he didn't push the button, there was a good chance someone higher up would order his execution anyway. To die now or to die later: that was the question.

10. DING.

9. DING.

Brooks looked at Smith, and Smith looked at Brooks. Smith glanced down at his holster and tilted his head, essentially asking for permission to wound the intern. Brooks shook his head.

8. DING.

Jimmy lunged for the button, expecting the worst. For a moment, the passengers felt like they were floating. Patience clutched Brooks's arm and began muttering a little prayer to herself. She thought wistfully about Salem; it seemed less dangerous at this point.

Luckily for Jimmy, the shrieking sound of the elevator's brakes working their hardest was followed not by violence but by mere exasperation.

"Jesus Christ, Jimmy," Smith said.

Patience gasped at the blasphemy.

When the elevator was fully stopped and no longer trembling, alarms began to ring. In fiction, there are two types of emergency alarms. The first is the low-pitched BROP BROP BROP found in nuclear meltdown scenarios. The second is a high-pitched BREEEP BREEEP BREEEP found when there's a security breach. The alarm at Reticent headquarters was neither of these. Because its agents faced peril nearly every day, alarming sounds were, frankly, not alarming to them. So it was decided that the emergency alarm would be a very pleasant TWINKLE TING TWINKLE TWINKLE TING. That cheery chime really got people's attention when they were buried in piles of dismembered corpses or, worse, piles of paperwork.

Jimmy puffed up his 28-inch chest and stood defiant. "You've gone rogue! I had to do something, or—"

"On the bright side," Brooks said, "you'll go down in history as the guy who stopped us from stopping the world from coming to an end."

"Of course history will only remember that for, what, a week?" Smith added.

"Wh-what?"

Smith shook his head. "You could have just asked, Jimmy. Jesus Christ."

Patience gasped again.

"*Agents Brooks and Smith*," Brooks said, with a pointed look.

Jimmy's jaw dropped. "Section 4.91.3? You guys stopped the Goblin King?"

"Yep," Smith said, "and now we're gonna be hauled away or shot."

"Thanks, Jimmy," Brooks added.

The intern was terrified. Whatever punishment existed for not reporting rogue agents had to be less than the punishment for aiding and abetting the apocalypse itself. He tried to think, but came up blank, other than *Ma was right. I should have gone into finance.*

"There has to be something we can do," Jimmy said.

Brooks tried to think and was, unlike Jimmy, successful. "There's an emergency exit on 8. East wing. A staircase that leads up to a utility tunnel. Of course that's useless if—"

They heard some muttering on the other side of the elevator door. There was definitely a group of agents just outside the elevator, ready to harm them. Smith punched Jimmy in the face, knocking the intern to the floor, where he held his bleeding nose and made whining noises.

"What the hell?" Brooks asked.

"Roll with it," Smith instructed.

The door opened, and six armed agents greeted them.

"What's going on here?" one of them asked, pointing a gun at Brooks's face. "Who pressed the emergency stop?"

Smith, now knelt over the hapless intern, did his best impression of someone experiencing panic. "There's something wrong with the intern," he said. "He started muttering to himself and bleeding from his nose. He's probably under mind control, if I had to guess."

Jimmy played along, thrashing against Smith and repeating the same phrase over and over. "We need to take Level 14. We need to take Level 14. We need to take Level 14." As the armed guards leaned closer, Jimmy began screaming. "LET ME GO! I NEED TO GET TO LEVEL 14!" It was an admirable performance, if one that would shortly see him dead.

As the intern continued thrashing, Smith pretended to be overpowered. The intern jumped up to leave the elevator and was immediately tackled by three of the guards. Another looked at Patience.

"And where are you taking her?"

"To Holding before the kid hijacked the elevator," Brooks said.

The guard leaned into the car, pressed 18, and Brooks,

Smith, and Patience were on their way, headed in the wrong direction.

9. DING.

10. DING.

11. DING.

12. DING.

Brooks stopped the car and shuffled Patience out onto Level 12: Extraterrestrial Affairs.

"What are you doing?" Smith asked, following.

"If we turn around and go up, what do you think the odds are those guys are waiting for us on 8?"

"Pretty high."

"I don't feel like a 2-on-6 gunfight today, do you?"

Some part of Smith really, really did.

"It could be fun," he said.

His partner ignored that. "There's another emergency exit this level, and the UFO freaks—"

"—Don't leave their cubicles very often," Smith finished. "Good call."

The hallways of Extraterrestrial Affairs were dimly lit, but the employees on that level still thought them too bright to traverse. It was better to stay in the light-free sanctity of their workspaces, illuminated only by computer monitors that displayed conspiracy websites and alleged flying saucer sightings. "Jet fuel can't melt steel beams," one screen displayed as the agents walked by and glanced through a tinted window.

"Jesus," Smith said.

Patience gasped.

"Stop taking the lord's name in vain, would you?" Brooks asked.

"Why? I thought you were over that shit—"

"You're freaking the kid out," Brooks said.

Smith snorted. "Like the time travel and disembowelment didn't do that already."

"Are you okay?" Brooks asked Patience, ignoring the snark.

Remembering her direction to be silent, Patience simply nodded.

All things considered, Patience was handling her new environment well. She was handling it freakishly quietly, but still well. It wasn't in her nature to be talkative and in this case there was almost certainly no need. Arthur and Edward, as she thought of them, seemed to be on the right side of things, and they seemed to know what they were doing. If Patience could have understood just how much the two men made up on the fly, she would have been terrified. But she couldn't, so she happily shuffled toward the emergency exit.

The utility tunnel led into a subway station. The three ascended the stairs to exit the station and Smith immediately stepped to the curb to hail a cab. A few drivers gave sideways glances at the young girl in a hospital gown and lab coat and kept driving. There was always at least one, though, who was willing to take on any fare. Namir Ahmad was one such driver. He had ferried couples in the middle of domestic disputes, saying nothing when they skirmished in the backseat. He had ferried mobsters whose luggage was obviously leaking suspicious fluids. He had ferried career politicians. No passenger was too foul. So when he saw two grown men with a sick teenager they'd obviously abducted, he pulled his car over and welcomed them aboard. That's not to say the driver approved, but he still owed $300,000 on his medallion and rideshares were ruining his business, so it was what it was.

The agents flanked Patience, who was not at all disappointed to have the disappointing middle seat. When the car moved forward, she gasped a little.

"Where to?" Namir asked.

"90 Bay Street Landing, Staten Island," Smith said. He noticed that their cab was not equipped with modern technology, and turned to Brooks with a shrug. "You have cash, right?"

"Yeah." Brooks sighed before muttering "*puta barata*" under his breath.

Smith incorrectly interpreted that as "pointy sweet potato."

Namir, meanwhile, grinned and shook his fist in triumph. Lower Manhattan to Staten Island was going to be one hell of a fare.

16 / THE STORM BEFORE THE STORM

"$81.16."

They'd been lucky and hit little traffic. Brooks reached into his wallet and pulled out five $20 bills. Namir pointed to a hand-scribbled sign that read "Driver does not make change." That didn't seem right to Brooks, but he knew he was in no position to argue.

The tear above Reticent headquarters had grown so large that it was visible from Staten Island. The gash, now roughly the size of Manhattan, hovered conveniently over Manhattan for scale. Within it was the same emptiness as before. No glow. No stars. Nothing. Brooks reflected that he had no desire to live in such a void, and left all of his money with the driver.

Namir sped away toward Manhattan. With people inevitably trying to escape the tear in reality, traffic leaving the city would soon pace at a crawl, and he wanted nothing more than to join that time and money-consuming congestion.

In the commotion, no one at Reticent headquarters was looking for the agents or for Patience. Brooks undid her cuffs and took her by the hand. As they headed for Hudson's apartment, Smith paused for a moment to stare at the rift. He found the nothingness pleasant in its own way. If it were to devour everything (he wasn't rooting for it), there would be no pain, no stress, and no inevitable horrific death sequence. He wouldn't turn on their mission, but if they failed to stop it, he figured there were worse things than simple nonexistence.

They barged into Hudson's locked apartment, expecting to find it empty. Instead, they found the man himself, hunched over his desk and staring at a large chunk of white marble.

"We got her," Brooks said. "Now what?"

Hudson swung his chair around to face them and put his hands in the air in an act of surrender. "Whatever you want, just take it."

Brooks and Smith exchanged baffled glances. Patience shuffled across the room and seated herself.

"We haven't met?" Brooks was again unsure whether to make that a statement or a question.

"Should we have?" Hudson asked, eyeing him up.

As the agents approached, it became clear that this Hudson was from 2014. Whereas the last time they'd met, Hudson's face had been a near match for the photo in his apartment, this time it was a perfect match.

"Is this about the machine?" Hudson asked. He stared at Smith for a moment. "Are we related?"

"Uh, no." Smith didn't know that was true. It was possible that Hudson Marrow had traveled back in time and slept with one of his ancestors, but the fact that Hudson Marrow was undesirable in nearly every way a human being can be undesirable suggested that probably wasn't the case. His overly nasal voice alone should have ensured his perpetual virginity, let alone the complete, mustard-stained Hudson Marrow package.

"Agents Brooks and Smith," Brooks said.

"Agents of what?" Hudson asked. "The FBI?"

"The Reticent," Smith said.

"Damn it, Eddie," Brooks said. Disclosing their secret organization didn't matter now that they had betrayed it, but he was still annoyed.

"The medical research firm?" Hudson asked. He stopped talking to them and began whispering to himself. "Of course. It's a front. I always did think that was a stupid name for a medical research firm..."

"I don't suppose you've noticed the giant hole over

Manhattan?" Smith asked.

"Hmm?" Hudson had been so absorbed in the piece of marble that he had not.

They directed him to take a look out his window and, sure enough, the gap now extended over the bay.

"What does this have to do with me?" Hudson asked.

"Your time machine caused a paradox," Brooks said.

The agents expected their no-longer-missing person to react with fear, outrage, or crippling depression at the notion that he had caused this disaster. They were disappointed when Hudson chuckled dismissively. "That's not even possible."

"What?" the agents said at once.

"You said it was," Brooks said.

"I've never talked to you before now," Hudson noted.

"Not you," Smith said, "Future you. 2090 you."

Hudson Marrow was no longer a physics professor, so he hadn't been as engaged in the current research as he would have liked, but he was reasonably certain that Brooks and Smith were incorrect. He had invented the time machine, after all. He should know how it worked.

"I don't know how it works," he said. "Not entirely. Time travel is as new to me as it is to you. But from what I've observed, it's a non-breakable loop, just as Einstein predicted. If you go back, you've always gone back. If you go forward, you've always gone forward. I've found pictures of myself in the 1800s that have apparently always been in historical records. You just don't understand all the pieces until you've lived them..."

"Okay, but you see the rift, right?" Brooks asked. "Future you probably knows more than current you, and that rift has to be caused by something."

"Sure, but not the time machine. I'm telling you. CTCs are the rule of the land," Hudson said.

"CTCs?" Smith wondered.

"Closed Timelike Curves," Brooks said, recalling one of his two physics courses.

"Which means...?"

"How much do you know about Lorentzian manifolds?" Hudson asked.

Smith didn't appreciate the condescending tone. He pointedly eyed the complete set of *Star Wars* posters on the wall and remarked, "About as much as you know about getting laid, I'd guess."

"You'd be surprised," Hudson mumbled. He glanced at the Puritan who had politely seated herself in the corner of the room. "I'm assuming you two are the ones who broke in here the other day?"

"How did you know someone was here?" Brooks asked.

"Somebody stole my lighter," Hudson said.

Brooks folded his arms and scowled at his partner. "Seriously?"

Hudson's brow furrowed. "That and I had to wash the sex smell out of my sheets."

Brooks unfolded his arms and blushed. Patience also blushed from across the room. She didn't understand the mechanics, but that wasn't a word people said aloud in her time.

"I'm also assuming," Hudson continued, "that you brought her here from the past."

"Yeah, and now we're here to fix it," Smith said.

Patience shot up. "You're going to force my return?"

"Hey, she does speak," Smith said. "Yes. We have to send you back."

"Well maybe not," Brooks said. "If the professor is right..."

"Oh, I'm not a professor anymore," Hudson said. "There was... an incident."

"An incident?" Smith asked.

"Nothing involving the machine, I assure you."

"Then what do you do now?" Brooks asked.

"I work in rock fraud for the Department of Consumer Affairs," Hudson said.

Smith couldn't think of anything sufficiently snarky to say in his bewilderment. "Rock fraud?"

"Yes. You see, marble is, legally speaking, metamorphosed limestone. A lot of stonemasons will sell un-metamorphosed limestone as marble, though, and charge for it accordingly. That's rock fraud." He followed that with a soft sigh that would be best translated as "I hate my job."

The agents were speechless, until Smith wasn't. "You're a rock jockey, and we're supposed to trust you on time travel?"

"Do you trust Einstein?" Hudson asked.

"Not really," Smith said.

Patience interrupted the silence that followed with an impassioned plea. "I don't wish to go back."

"Can we find out what happened to her, historically?" Brooks asked.

"Yeah, sure."

Hudson no longer had tenure, but he still had his research skills and subscriptions to every academic search imaginable. Within a few minutes he had pulled up a detailed history of what happened to everyone who had lived in Salem during the witchcraft trials. Patience stood over his shoulder, in awe of the nearly instantaneous information.

"It says here she disappeared on August 3rd, 1692 and was never heard from again."

"Is August 3rd the day we picked you up?" Brooks asked.

"Yes, sir." She remembered Smith's request that she go sir-free. "That is... Yes. It was."

"That fits with that I've seen so far," Hudson said. "You always brought her here."

"Then why did future you lie to us?" Smith asked, gesturing out the window. "And what's causing all of that? You think it's just a coincidence it started when she showed up?"

The tear was still expanding. Everyone in the room gathered around the window to watch as it reached over the Statue of Liberty. Then, as quickly as it had opened, the anomaly shrank and closed without a sound. The skyline returned to normal without Brooks and Smith doing a damn thing.

17 / TIME GOES BY

Inside Reticent headquarters, Charlotte Nguyen entered the Brooks/Smith office and began shouting expletives, as had been foretold. On Brooks's desk was a piece of 92 bright copy paper with an SD card atop it and a pink post-it note affixed. The note said: "Return to Agatha Werewith." There was a smiley face at the bottom. That was Smith's idea.

Nguyen fumed to her boss, who fumed to his boss above him, and somewhere along the line, someone fumed to Werewith herself. That fuming necessitated another meeting in *the* conference room. This one was bigger than the last and involved a lot more berating of low-level management.

"I thought," Werewith said, "that agents Brooks and Smith were our best."

"They are," Nguyen said. "That's why we never did anything about—"

"About their *camaraderie*, yes." Werewith paused. "Do you know why they took the girl?"

"Yes, ma'am. Agent Brooks called and said something about a time paradox, but I told him that couldn't happen and that we weren't interested..."

Werewith leaned over the table. "And you didn't think to elevate that conversation to anyone else here?"

"I had no reason to believe they would act on it," Nguyen said. "Brooks is a model agent and Smith... well, he wouldn't do it alone"

"Well, it's a good thing your instincts are so solid."

Nguyen's face froze and she swallowed hard. She knew exactly what happened to agents who displeased Agatha Werewith.

"You're done," Werewith said.

"No," Nguyen pleaded. "I'll bring them back. I'll figure out what they did with the girl and bring all three of them back."

"No, you won't." Werewith smiled and spoke in a cheery tone. "You're done here."

When the Reticent CEO said that someone was "done," she meant it. Agents could, of course, be fired. In that case they would simply lose their benefits and, if they were privy to any particularly sensitive information, have it erased from their memories. Agents who had committed grievous errors (such as, say, wronging someone at the top of the chain) had everything erased—not just memories of monsters, aliens, and cybernetic uprisings, but their identities, histories, and personalities. When the mindwipe was complete, what remained was a shell of a human being, often comatose, who would never bother anyone again. Sometimes, for good measure, even their faces were altered. That part wasn't necessary, but it was entertaining. A favorite trick of Agatha's was to have them made to look like Nicholas Cage in homage to the movie *Face/Off.*

Agent Nguyen was restrained by two guards and escorted out of the room. Once she was done screaming at the conference room, nobody would ever hear from her again. The screaming lasted for some time, though. Werewirth impatiently tapped her fingernails on the table.

"Don't do this! Please!"

The fingernails continued their dance.

"Pllleeeaaaaaaaaaase!"

In the distance, a door slammed shut, and the conference room went silent, except for the tapping. Werewith tilted her head and put a hand to her ear, pretending to listen for more screams. When there was nothing, she continued.

"Now that that unpleasantness is taken care of, shall we talk about that rift?"

Nobody disagreed.

"When it's there, it's getting bigger, and it doesn't seem to be stable. Can someone tell me why?"

"We're looking into it," one of the suits said.

Another nodded. "We were hoping the Puritan would offer some insight, but—"

A third man nodded.

Werewith scowled at the man who had nothing to offer but a nod. She made a mental note that if there were one more strike against him, he'd be the next to go.

"Be better at your jobs," Werewith said. "This organization is in the red and we need that portal to get back in the black."

18 / SO SLOWLY

Patience had been instructed to stand and wait. She hovered over the Sunbeam 2-slice toaster, in awe of its glowing coils. When it popped, she practically fell over.

"It's ready?" she asked, catching her breath.

"Go for it," Hudson said.

With the rift closed, everyone had huddled in Hudson's breakfast nook, where the scientist attempted to explain the physics and mechanics behind his invention. That was of no interest to Arturo Brooks, not now. He was stuck on what Hudson said earlier about the timeline never changing. Smith could predict his partner's next question before he asked it, and his heart began racing.

"What if I decided right now to go back and save my father and sister from dying?" Brooks asked.

"If you could do it, it would have already happened," Hudson said.

That answer didn't satisfy the detective. "If everything is already predetermined, then what's the point?" Brooks asked, wondering the same thing millions of freshman philosophy students and stoners had wondered before him.

"You're misunderstanding. Your actions always have and always will affect what happens next."

"You just said everything has already happened."

"No. Everything *is* happening," Hudson said. "Every moment is linked and it's all happening at once. The Declaration of Independence is being signed right now. The sun is exploding and taking the Earth with it right now. Whatever you choose to do next is happening right now. That's what makes time travel so easy, really. You just have to find the spot you want on a very stationary map."

"Then I'm going back," Brooks announced.

Smith cringed. "Brooksy... that's... not a great idea."

"I'm going back." Brooks's tone announced that this was not up for debate. "If I always go back and save them, then they're alive right now. Right?"

Hudson nodded. In theory, that was correct. It was a dumb theory, though.

"And then I'll find out where and—"

"But they *aren't* alive," Smith said, dropping a hard dose of reality. "We can deduce *that* from the fact that they haven't looked for you at *any point* in the last ten years." He considered what Hudson had just told them: time wasn't breakable. That meant he could tell Brooks what he had been holding back for so long. But he couldn't bring himself to trust the rock fraud analyst he'd just met over his own eyes and the words of his future self.

Brooks refused to be anything less than optimistic. "The Reticent makes sure its agents are people with no close family. People who are traumatized. Maybe they kept them from me all this time. Maybe..."

Smith snapped and made his fear perfectly clear. "*Maybe* you go back and die a horrible death right there with them."

"If that's what you think is going to happen, come with me," Brooks said.

Smith shook his head. "No. Don't put that shit on me. Then if you die it's my fault I couldn't stop it."

"*Que sera sera.* If you don't come and I die you're going to think the same thing."

"Oh, screw you." Smith paced back and forth, practically pulling his hair out, wondering whether or not he went with his partner the last time this happened. "This is why time travel is against the rules. They're dead. They are supposed to be dead."

Those words stung. *Supposed to be dead.* Brooks shook his head. "I'm going," he said, stepping into the machine. "That is, if you don't mind..."

Hudson shrugged. "It won't hurt anything. On a cosmic scale, anyway."

Smith punched a hole in the drywall and let out a furious shout that startled everyone in the room.

"*I* mind!" he said.

Hudson threw up his hands and sighed at the damage.

Brooks stepped toward his partner. "I know you'll never understand what it's like to have a real family, but if you did and you had a chance to save them, you would. What if it were me?"

"I'd go back for you," Smith said. The same words kept repeating in his thoughts. *He can never know. He said he could never know. I said...* He pulled himself together and muttered "you're an idiot" before removing his bloodied hand from the wall and following his partner into the time machine.

"Just... wait," Smith said, putting his non-bloodied hand over his partner's.

"Why?" Brooks asked.

"Because I said so?" Smith had nothing.

"You're the one who says I've gotten lame," Brooks said. "So let's go."

"What if you die?" Smith asked.

"You'll fix it," Brooks said.

"I'll—" Smith stared, slack jawed.

"I've seen you do crazier things," Brooks said. He turned to Hudson. "Help me put in the right numbers."

Hudson groaned and rose from the couch.

Patience observed all of this in relative silence; the only sound that came from her direction was the crunching of toast. That lasted until the awful whirring sound returned, accompanied by the green flash.

*
**

Within minutes, the agents landed in the midst of chaos.

Wraiths at a music festival. The peace-loving crowd had even less a chance than the average person at deflecting the undead horde. Brooks was the first to take an unsteady step out of the time machine. The smell of the wraiths' decaying flesh hit him first, followed by a smell not unlike an old jar of pennies. So much human blood had been sprayed about that a metallic odor permeated the air. Brooks's breathing and heartbeat became rapid in unison. He saw a grey blur, felt a splash of blood hit his face, and realized he couldn't handle this.

Just as Brooks was about to enter fuck mode, Smith violently tugged his partner toward him. His other hand held the bloody knife that decapitated the wraith.

"Wake up," Smith said. "You came, you saw, you nearly passed out. Let's go."

Brooks faltered. "It's worse than I remember..." He regretted this. He wanted to go home. But he wasn't going to say that. If there was even the slightest chance he could save his family, he was going to take it.

Their time machine had landed near the main stage where the attack began. On the plus side, most of the wraiths had moved outward. On the other hand, this was the area hit hardest, as the bodies hadn't had the chance to spread out. Corpses, mostly adorned in tie dyed shirts, were piled on top of each other. One old man was slumped back in his folding chair, the blood from his torn throat gushing down into the margarita glass he still clutched. On the ground next to him was a still-smoldering joint. Brooks recognized him as his chemistry professor, Gene Adkins. He was going to bring his granddaughter, and, sure enough, nearby was the torso of an eight-year-old girl. Brooks choked back some vomit.

"We need to get to the carousel," Brooks said, his head

spinning.

"*Or*," Smith said, "we could get the hell out of here."

Brooks grabbed his pistol and made a run in the right direction, each step more defiant than the last. He still regretted this. He still wanted to go home. As he broke across the park, he saw them from afar: his father, his sister, and his younger self. An hour ago, they had been happy. Both he and Tasha were nearing their college graduations and she had recently become engaged. They had snacked on sandwiches and listened to folk rock. Not now.

There was an abundance of dumpsters on Staten Island, and one positioned right next to the Willowbrook Park carousel was just the right height to grant access to the attraction's roof. The Brooks family had climbed atop it, hoping to reach safety. As three wraiths circled the dumpster, his father gave the young Brooks a boost onto the roof of the carousel.

His lungs burning, the older Brooks knew two things: that he needed to exercise more and that he wasn't going to make it in time.

"Grab her hand," his father directed, giving Tasha a boost. She was too short to reach the roof without her brother's assistance.

The young Brooks reached out a hand, but before he could help her up she was ripped from his arms. The three wraiths pulled Norman Brooks to the ground and Tasha came toppling down with him. The wraiths dismembered her, first one arm, then the other.

Brooks looked away. He recalled the crunching, cracking, and slurping sounds his younger self was currently enduring for the first time. He was still fifty feet away, sprinting, thinking he could at least save his father. Half success would be better than no success.

No such luck. One of the monsters that killed his sister grabbed his father by the neck and ripped his throat out.

Brooks skidded to the ground and let out a pitiful yelp.

Thirty feet away, his younger self screamed as he jumped off the carousel roof, shocked and ready to die. He stared into one creature's yellow eyes and told it to fuck itself. As it lunged toward him, Agent Burroughs shot it in the head. Young Smith did the same to the other two wraiths as his Brooks dropped down, crying and praying. From that moment, their futures were set.

The older Smith leaned down next to the older Brooks as he gasped and choked.

"I'm sorry," Smith said.

"You knew about this..."

"I did. I'm sorry," Smith said.

"I'm sorry too," Agent Burroughs said. Her unsteady voice and her knife came from nowhere, and with a stab to the heart, Arturo Brooks was dead. Not physically—that would come in the next minute or two—but he was a dead man. Burroughs slinked away, saying something about orders.

"You...?" Smith started, but his former partner was already gone. He'd been watching and listening for wraiths, but the realization hit: it wasn't wraiths. It had never been wraiths. His younger self should have recognized a stab wound; it was so different from a mauling. He felt like an idiot. He was an idiot.

Brooks landed on his stomach, where he made an awful choking sound before losing consciousness. Even knowing his partner was a dead man, Smith rolled him over and made a pathetic attempt to revive him. There was blood everywhere. Smith put his hands on his partner's chest, trying to cover the wound, and pressed down. *It doesn't even work this way*, he thought as he performed CPR for no reason. *It doesn't even work this way.*

He removed his lips from his partner's for the last time and stared at his blood-drenched hands and shirt.

"Brooksy," he choked. "I'm sorry."

Edward Smith did nothing half-assedly, and grieving was no exception. The sounds he made drew his younger self to him.

"Hey, you're gonna be fine," the young man said.

"Get the fuck out of here," Smith said to himself.

The younger Smith recognized the face of the dead man as that of Arturo Brooks, the young man he had just met and saved. It took him an extra second to recognize himself.

This had always happened and it always would happen. The older Smith remembered what Hudson had said about time travel. There was nothing he could do to stop this.

"Don't say a word to Brooks," he said. "He can never know…"

He didn't mean it the way it came out, like a demand, like time and space would collapse if his younger self didn't follow the instruction. He just meant to not let Brooks see this. If it had to happen (and it did, according to Hudson), it was better a surprise. The words he said became stuck in his mind and he repeated them. His younger self, well aware of the Reticent's time travel rules, backed away, and Smith was again alone. He wished he had said something different. He wished for a drink. It occurred to him that he could go back again and clarify what he meant. He could do that, except he had never received such a clarification so he knew it would be futile.

Smith had known this day would come for ten years. He knew it at their first hookup. He knew it when he tried to remain distant the first few years of their partnership. He knew it when he fell in love.

He knew it every time he was a total asshole, and it had occurred to him on several occasions that if he could either a) drink his feelings away or b) drive Brooks away, everything would be fine.

He never managed to do either. Brooks was too perfectly forgiving, that stupid son of a bitch. Every day for a decade,

Smith watched as the reflection in the mirror became closer and closer to the man he'd seen before, and it made him angrier still. *He can never know.* Smith made sure of it. Brooks never knew that he always had been and always would be doomed.

Smith tried to stand up and call out to his younger self—to correct his language and fix this—but he was paralyzed. All he could think about was Brooks, and that there was no fixing this.

He slid his arm underneath his partner's, lifting him and leaning the sopping body against his shoulder. He had to at least get him back to 2014. He couldn't leave him to be disposed of with all the "krokodil addicts." He couldn't leave him where other members of the Reticent would find him. He turned back toward where they'd left the time machine and hobbled forward.

He saw two things: a second time machine and a blond figure pointing a gun at him. Smith wasn't sure whether this was real or he was delusional.

"What *now*?" he said to no one.

He never felt the bullet pierce his forehead.

19 / TIME COP OUT

While the 2014 versions of Brooks and Smith were lying dead on Staten Island in the year 2004, their 2007 selves were being handed their first assignment together. Brooks appeared in the doorway of the office Smith had shared with Burroughs for years, his arms folded and his mind agitated. Of course, he hadn't really been in a good mood in nearly three years. Joining the Reticent was supposed to help him get revenge on the kinds of creatures that killed his family. Instead, he spent a hell of a lot of time doing paperwork.

He noted the packed boxes scattered around the office and had to peek behind one to find his new partner.

"I thought we were supposed to meet upstairs," Brooks snapped.

Smith didn't look up from his computer. "Yeah, we are."

"...Forty five minutes ago."

"*Shit.*" Smith jumped from his seat and grabbed his coat. He needed a few more minutes to finish what he was working on, but the crossed arms told him not to request the extra time. "Yeah, let's go."

It was a decently long walk to Battery Park, even at their hurried 'It's March in New York and I'm going to freeze to death' paces, and the two had a decently long conversation as they walked it.

"So, the Reticent working out for you?" Smith asked.

"Seems like it, but why am I here? Your partner wasn't working out for you?" Brooks asked.

Smith's mouth tilted. "I wouldn't say that."

Brooks let out an exaggerated gasp. "You didn't."

"If you're insinuating that I violated rule 1.14.9 with my partner, you are correct. If you're thinking that it happened in our office, you are also correct. If, by some chance, you're suggesting that I did a thing that she really didn't like, which led to her shouting at me, which led to our boss finding out and ending our partnership... Yes. That happened."

"And neither of you were fired?" Brooks asked, in disbelief. There was something strangely attractive in how nonchalant his new partner was about the whole thing.

"*Demoted*," Smith said. "That's why I'm babysitting you."

Brooks was at the very end of his initial probationary period. If the next three months proceeded without incident, he would become a full-fledged agent. Under his new partnership, the odds of the next three months proceeding without incident had just decreased tenfold. He didn't know that, of course, but he did know that he found himself far too distracted by Smith's eyes. *It should be illegal to have eyes that green...* He cut that thought off before it was fully formed; gazing at his new partner would be a great way to never make it past the probationary period.

"So what's your deal?" Smith asked. "You got a boyfriend?"

Brooks, stunned, failed to respond.

"Girlfriend?" Smith asked, perplexed.

"No, you got it right the first time. But no. There's nobody." Brooks paused. "How did you—"

Smith gave himself a mental high five. "Please. You are too gorgeous to be straight. Also, you keep staring at my eyes like we're in a Fabio-covered romance novel." Brooks turned bright red, and Smith winked. "Lucky for me."

And just like that, the conversation became tense, even as it turned to the mission. "So this guy in Battery Park..." Brooks said, pretending to focus on work.

"He sells potions, amulets, and whatnot. Six days a week. Huge hit with the tourists," Smith said.

There was well-founded suspicion that the potions and amulets were, at least in part, real magical artifacts. That was a problem, and that was why they were investigating.

"Yeah, I know," Brooks said. "I read the file. I was gonna ask if you know how late he works."

"I think he's usually there all day, 'til 6 at least."

Brooks looked at his watch. 2PM. "You want to get something to eat first, then?"

Smith came to a halt, very nearly causing the woman walking behind him to rear end him. She muttered something explicit as she dodged him at the last second, but Smith was too startled to hear. He pressed his back against a building to get out of the way and Brooks followed.

"Are you hitting on me?" Smith asked.

Brooks shrugged.

"I was just demoted for workplace relations—"

"Yeah, so obviously you're up for some."

"Holy shit." Smith knew that this poor, pitiful fool was going to end up dead in Willowbrook Park, but he was a poor, pitiful, ridiculously attractive fool, and that made all the difference.

"Have you been to MacGuffin's?" Brooks asked. "They make this braised pork sandwich—"

"I'll take a raincheck on lunch," Smith said, taking his new partner's hand and pulling him into a narrow alley. Actually dating Brooks would be completely pointless. "But if—"

He didn't have time to finish the sentence. Brooks pressed him against the wall and, with no warning, they were kissing. It was the second most intense make out session of Smith's life, and who could ever compare with Mick Jagger? With less than no warning, Brooks dropped to his knees. His breath made a thin stream in the cold air. Then there was the sound of his own zipper, and Smith was treated to a much better sight than condensation.

***

Smith woke up thinking about that moment, back when Brooks was alive. Back when he himself was alive. Smith rolled his stiff neck as he realized that he actually was still alive. That fact left him partly confused but mostly disgruntled. The room was dark, and he was lying on his back. An attempt to sit up was met with failure. Tight leather straps kept his chest from going anywhere. He writhed back and forth, trying to free his arms from his sides. When that didn't work, he leaned his head back and exhaled rapidly. Being tied up was, for him, what visiting Staten Island was for Brooks. That is to say he was on the verge of a very loud, very explicit meltdown.

A thin strand of light stretched across the room, and Smith could suddenly hear voices.

"Yeah, he's still out," one said.

"It's not the time machine?" asked another.

"Can't be. The other one used it and he died."

Hearing his partner referred to as 'the other one' made Smith writhe harder.

"Well, that puts a wrench in our plans."

"It does. But we can still toss this one into the empty and see what happens."

Smith was fed up. "Hey, assholes!" he yelled. "Untie me!"

With that, the room flooded with light. Everything went white and yellow, and Smith was temporarily blinded. He could feel one of the men tightening the straps against his chest while the other rifled through a metal cabinet on the other side of the room. The cabinet shut with a CLANG. Smith kept shouting expletives, not knowing where or at whom they were directed.

Then Smith's eyes began to focus on an employee badge dangling in front of him. He could just make out some color: blue and purple on the left, yellow on the right. Everything was blurry, but he knew what he was dealing with. The colors were in the right positions for Reticent badges, and he cursed them loudly. There was a sharp pain in Smith's right arm, and he felt his skin getting warmer. Then everything went black again.

20 / TIMELY APPOINTMENT

Hudson Marrow had built a contingency plan into his time machine. It was quantum locked to him, and if the people inside didn't return it to his present day within twenty-four hours, the pod would automatically return itself. Presented with company for the first time in a long time, he had tried explaining this to Patience. She looked at him like he was speaking Dutch and didn't say a word in response.

After waiting three hours for the agents' return, he had a suspicion he would be waiting twenty-four hours for an empty machine. He didn't know what had happened to them, and he wasn't particularly fussed about it. He didn't know them, after all. What did interest him was that the rift over Manhattan had returned to his apartment's vista. It hadn't grown since he'd last seen it, but a giant empty void couldn't mean anything good was about to happen, if sci-fi books were anything to go on.

Worse than the rift, the agents had left Hudson with a Puritan girl who sat silently and creepily, fascinated by the news program he'd turned on to mitigate the creepy silence. Hudson tried to focus on the potentially fraudulent rock in front of him, but was disquieted by Patience's silence. He was equally disquieted when she finally spoke.

"Excuse me, sir," she said.

"Hmm?"

"Am I to understand that you do not serve the crown?"

"No. You've missed about three hundred and twenty years of history. You're in the United States of America. It's been a separate nation since 1776. Or '81. Or '88, really, depending on how you look at it."

She paid no attention to his wavering, but proceeded with another question. "Who is Kim Kardashian?"

"That's not really important," Hudson said.

The news begged to differ. The barely informative programming made way for a commercial break. Anticipating a slew of questions about cars, car insurance, *The Bachelor*, and medication for erectile dysfunction, Hudson grabbed the remote and turned the television off. He was already on edge due to an impending appointment. He didn't need this.

"Tell you what," he said. "I'll put in some movies about the history of the United States. How does that sound?"

"That sounds delightful," she said.

Hudson cringed. There was something eerie about a teenage girl who used the word 'delightful.' She was too functional for a regular teen, let alone one who had been ripped from the past and dropped onto Staten Island. Regardless, he put the movie on and brought the girl a glass of water and a bag of microwaved popcorn.

"Is this really food?" Patience asked.

Hudson nodded.

"Is everything here eaten out of a bag?" she asked, recalling the grilled cheese sandwich that had eluded her.

"Not everything, no."

She tasted a kernel and curled her lip in disgust. "Is everything here this salty?"

Hudson considered that for a moment and shrugged. "Yes."

A rapid, angry knock at the front door told him that his appointment had come. KNOCKOCKOCKOCK. It didn't give him enough time to answer the door before it repeated. KNOCKOCKOCKOCK. He buried his face in his hands and told Patience to be quiet for a while.

KNOCKOCKOCKOCK.

Hudson's soon-to-be ex-wife, Veronica, greeted him with a frown.

"Took you long enough," she huffed.

"Now is not a good time," he said, stretching across the

doorway in an effort to keep her in the hallway.

Like her husband, Veronica Marrow was in her fifties. Unlike her husband, her appearance was age appropriate. She had grey hair and a dignified look about her—one that didn't involve a stained t-shirt. Had agents Brooks and Smith been alive to see her, they would have recognized her as the woman in the Stanley Cup photo. Then Brooks would have been forced to apologize for Smith making a remark about how she looked old enough to be Hudson's mother.

"We need to go over the papers," Veronica said, moving from side to side trying to get around him. "You said today."

"I think the anomaly over the city counts as reason enough not to do it today," Hudson said.

Veronica shook her head. "I don't think so."

Hudson had been delaying this divorce as long as possible, and now that they were entering year two of the proceedings, Veronica was over niceties. She pushed past him and into the messy apartment, where she found hundreds of ancient artifacts she'd never seen before.

"When did you get all of this?" she demanded. "None of this was in your asset list."

"I told you, now is not a good time to—"

Her reasonable demeanor completely changed when she saw the teenage girl nibbling popcorn on the couch. "You have *got* to be kidding me! Coeds aren't young enough for you now?"

"That's not—"

"Actual teenagers!" she exclaimed, then turned to Patience. "Do your parents know where you are?"

"No, ma'am," answered the Puritan.

"Don't get funny with me," Veronica said, unimpressed with the girl's polite response. She turned to Hudson. "You're right. Now *isn't* a good time. I'll be back with my attorney to review all the assets you've been *hiding*."

Hudson's mind worked faster than his mouth, and he

stumbled over his words. "I don't... I haven't been hiding them. It's not—"

Veronica was rightly tired of Hudson's tired excuses. In this case, he wasn't lying, but historically speaking that was the exception rather than the rule. She stormed out of the apartment, advising Patience to "get out of this mess."

Patience wasn't sure what the commotion was about, but she had come to enjoy the popcorn.

21 / PURE PURITANISM

The people of Salem, Massachusetts did not enjoy what was happening to them. After Patience walked away from the undertaker, John Wilmington (the man previously charged with killing her) had been sentenced to die. Obviously, the magistrate decided, Mr. Wilmington had performed some sort of witchcraft on the noose that hanged her to render it ineffective. Alternately, he had used magic to grant her immunity to being strangled. Whatever it was, he had to have done something wrong because Patience Cloyce had not stayed dead.

After Mr. Wilmington's execution, he too had awoken at the undertaker's. That, in turn, had led the townspeople to blame the undertaker's assistant, Clemency. Obviously, the magistrate decided, he had learned some sort of witchcraft that resurrected people. Alternately, he had made a deal with the devil. Whatever it was, he had to have done something wrong since John Wilmington had not stayed dead.

After the undertaker's assistant's execution, he too had awoken at his own place of business. That, in turn, had led the townspeople to an undead end. The next logical course for the townspeople was that the magistrate had learned some sort of witchcraft and, when he sentenced people to die, had really been sentencing them to live forever. Alternately, someone else was scheming against the magistrate. Whatever it was, he had to have done something wrong and he had to die.

After the magistrate's execution, he too had awoken at the undertaker's. The people of Salem, in their decidedly finite wisdom, decided that, if the rules of death no longer applied, they had no choice but to punish everyone. The town itself must have betrayed God in some way and now they were being reborn so they could serve more faithfully. They arranged a public gathering, during which each townsperson would kill another.

Stan Sanford—now technically the first President of the United States—walked into town during that gathering. He glanced down at three dead Puritans and curled his lip in disgust.

"Excuse me," he said to one who was tying a rope around her neck.

"Sir?" she wondered.

"Can you direct me to the person in charge around here?" Stan asked.

"That would be Mr. William Stoughton, sir. He's the head magistrate." She gestured down the street to where the magistrate—in a meandrous powdered wig that was somehow both flamboyant and somber—was in the process of pressing a local farmer to death.

As Stan approached, the townspeople put a pause on all the murder and stared at him. Somewhere along the way, Stan's ruff had fallen off, and they had never seen someone in the official uniform of Luna: a grey jumpsuit with a star-shaped medallion pinned to the chest. Stan had designed and approved that uniform himself and was very proud of it, but it didn't help him here, where outsiders were at best feared and at worst killed. He approached the magistrate with little worry.

"I need to speak with you," Stan said. "Has anything strange been happening around here?"

Stoughton blinked. "The strangest thing that's happened so far is your appearance."

Soon, the outsider found himself surrounded by vengeful Puritans. Stan sighed. They were going to insist on doing this the hard way. He could take it, of course, but he wasn't happy about it.

After his lynching and subsequent resurrection, Stan dusted himself off and confronted the magistrate again.

"That was no way to treat a visitor," he said.

Stoughton didn't care for hospitality. "I see you're afflicted as well. I don't suppose you could explain what's happening around here..."

"Afflicted?" Stan wondered. "How many others are like me?"

The magistrate's answer was vague. "Some. Fewer are afflicted than aren't afflicted, it seems. Most of the people who've died these last two days have stayed dead."

Stan mumbled under his breath. "I don't remember that in the history books..."

"I beg your pardon?"

"Nothing."

The massacre was welcome news. Not for the town of Salem, which had quickly found itself decimated by mass suicide and homicide, but for the future of humanity itself. Most people, Stan reflected, were supposed to stay dead.

22 / TWICE IN A LIFETIME

Twenty-four hours after agents Brooks and Smith left 2014 for 2004, Hudson Marrow's time machine reappeared in his bedroom, empty.

"Looks like they didn't make it back," he said, expecting no response.

Patience did not respond.

The void had disappeared and reappeared a half dozen times overnight. Hudson suspected, based on its epicenter, that it had something to do with the medical research firm/top secret organization for which the agents had worked. When he scouted Reticent headquarters a few hours earlier, it was swarming with people dressed just like the two dead men. Far too dangerous for a rock jockey. Hudson had no plans to take either himself or the girl inside the building, and the only other lead he had at this point was his future self. Brooks had mentioned speaking with him before and, on a curious note, Hudson really wanted to meet the version of himself who had managed to age, however slightly.

With that in mind, he set his destination to 2090 and prepared for takeoff. Then he remembered Patience and debated whether to bring or leave her. She certainly wouldn't be of use in the future, but if he left her, the odds the Reticent would come knocking were high. So he decided to bring her along. Hudson gave her one of Veronica's more modest dresses to wear, but Patience was still embarrassed by its cap sleeves.

"Must I appear in public like this?" she asked.

"You can stay in the machine if you'd like," he said. "But I don't recommend staying here."

Patience nodded.

"Don't touch anything," he directed as he motioned her

into the machine ahead of him.

She wouldn't have dared.

Hudson hopped in behind her, fidgeted with a few dials, and the intense shaking began. Then the loud whirring noise. Then the green glow. The others who had used the time machine probably hadn't realized it, but that glow was caused by radioactive isotopes. That might have given them pause. Hudson considered whether he should have told them that.

Oh well, he thought. *They're dead.*

He had no idea where in the future he should land, so he aimed for his own apartment. When the space-time pudding gave way to the sound of a woman shrieking and calling for her wife, Hudson reasoned that, in 2090, he no longer lived there. In fact, it wasn't even the same building. Whereas his own apartment complex was twelve stories high, this one was twenty-eight. All of the buildings in every direction seemed to have doubled in size. He wanted nothing more than to explore the premises and see what sorts of technology the future held, but he'd already attracted too much attention and didn't need the police or robocops or whatever protected and served the day after him. In a very real sense, he needed to find himself.

After moving the time machine out of the more well-populated areas and onto a docked boat, he was ready to begin his search. The internet, he found, still worked about the same as it had in the past, and it didn't take long to get his tablet connected to some free future Wi-Fi, "sponsored by IntelliSprint and brought to you by Taco Bell." After enduring two minutes of mandatory ad viewing (double-stuffed faux meat volcano quesaritos were back, apparently), he sprawled out in the boat's cabin, ready to begin his research.

"Excuse me..."

Hudson had nearly forgotten that Patience was with him. Annoyed, he looked up from the Microsoft x Disney search engine collab the WiFi had automatically redirected him to.

"*What?*" he snipped.

The Puritan entered from the deck with wide eyes. "The sky appears to be turning to nothing again."

Sure enough, when he peeked outside, Hudson saw the rift. Whether it was only in the year 2090 or across time, he could not say. He could only be in one place at a time and one time at a place, for now. If he could find his future self, he could be in two places at once and that would be helpful in solving their mystery. Maybe.

Google, presented by AOLTimeNewscorp, revealed that Hudson Marrow was famous. "The Immortal Man" had written dozens of books about his experiments and experiences alike, and they seemed to be quite popular. Of course, some of the results were from conspiracy-peddling "Nomortalers" who thought that he was lying about his condition or "Nobominationers" who thought that he was literally the antichrist. It was bittersweet to see that the internet hadn't really changed.

He, on the other hand, had changed a lot. Three years ago, said the sources, he went into full reclusivity and moved to upstate New York. He had only been spotted a dozen times since, each time fatter and with more facial hair than the last. The idea of having a midlife crisis at age 127 nearly sent him into a midlife crisis at age 50. But there might have been another explanation, so he carried on to upstate New York.

Normally, a home the size of 2090 Hudson Marrow's would come with staff—maids, gardeners, a guard at the front gate—but the home's occupant wanted nothing to do with them. Aside from occasional interviews and appearances at charity events, he desired solitude. So when 2014 Hudson Marrow and Patience Cloyce arrived at the front gate, there was nothing stopping them from slipping inside. Patience looked up at the enormous home with thick marble columns and decided that future Hudson ruled over at least three colonies, perhaps an entire province.

Hudson gingerly reached for the brass door handle. To his surprise, it was unlocked. He never left his apartments unlocked; he couldn't imagine he would leave a mansion in such a state. There were too many precious artifacts, too many marble slabs, too many time machines. There was only one time machine, but still. That was one too many to risk thievery. He pushed the door open and there wasn't even a security alarm.

Hudson snorted in disbelief before calling out, "Hello?"

A familiar figure, wearing only an open bathrobe, meandered into the foyer from behind a marble column. Patience looked away, blushing.

"About time," the man said.

Hudson eyed his future self from top to bottom.

"You're not me," he said.

It was the regrettable pelvic tattoo—a Chinese-style dragon with the words 'No Fear' scribbled above it—that gave it away.

"No shit," said the man from 2090. "You ready to take over again or what?"

Hudson squinted. "Excuse me?"

Some things didn't change over the course of seventy-five years. When he realized that the man he was talking to was not the Hudson Marrow of his time, Edward Smith tied his robe shut and articulated his frustration in his usual manner.

"Fuck," he said.

There was a very long, very boring conversation between the two men. It revealed the following: after Hudson Marrow became a celebrity thanks to his immortality, the public tracked him as if he were royalty. There were paparazzi. There were more events than he could handle, and all he really wanted to do was perform more science experiments. So he had an idea. He sought an old acquaintance who looked a lot like him. Hudson began to put on weight. Smith, in turn, put on a lot of weight (and though he bitched about it, he greatly enjoyed the process). Hudson became reclusive. The public, no longer getting frequent glimpses of him, didn't notice when the switch was made. Hudson took the alias Stan Sanford and headed for Texas to work at a space exploration company. Smith took the alias Hudson Marrow and resumed a few of the man's public activities. Very few.

"I've been trying to get you—future you—here for months," Smith said. "I'm tired of this bullshit."

"Yeah, looks like you live a rough life," Hudson said, glancing around the mansion.

"I thought being someone else would help. It didn't. Now I'm done."

"Well, I'm sorry I haven't shown up," Hudson said. "Maybe I'm dead?"

Smith responded with scorn. "We both know that's not the case."

"Pardon me," Patience said. "I don't mean to interrupt, but in my time there was a letter from Mr. Hudson Marrow that apologized to someone named Stan." She knew it wasn't Satan, and wished she could rub that fact into her parents' faces. Then she felt ashamed.

"Yeah, I wrote that," Smith said. "I left copies all over the place in hopes this time-traveling jackass would notice and come back."

"You left things in the past?" Hudson asked. "What's wrong with you?"

"Hey, you're the one who said it wasn't possible to break history," said Smith.

"I said it didn't *seem* possible. Thorough research could conclude something diff—"

"Whatever. I don't care. I did find something else out, though." Smith paused. "Every time I travel through time, I get a little bit older."

"Okay, so..."

"So whatever makes us immortal, we can beat it."

"You're immortal too?" Hudson asked.

Smith shrugged. "Yeah."

"Then why didn't you come back from 2004?" Hudson asked. "The time machine came back empty—"

"Long story." Smith's face let Hudson know he wouldn't discuss it.

"Well, that makes three of us," Hudson said, glancing at Patience. "But why would you want to 'beat it'?"

"Why wouldn't you?" Smith asked.

"By 'beating it,' you mean *dying*, right?"

"No, I'm talking about pumping the python." Smith rolled his eyes. "Yeah, I mean dying."

Patience silently wondered how snakes were relevant to the conversation.

"I don't want to die," Hudson said. "Why would anyone? Do you know how many things you could experience in multiple lifetimes? How much accumulated knowledge you—"

"Yeah, you say that now. Why don't you try another hundred years and we'll talk," said Smith.

"You already know the me who's lived for a hundred years, and he left to do more research. Not to kill himself."

"Shut up. Maybe not a hundred, but you know what I mean. Try two hundred. Try three. Try a thousand. You think it's gonna be a hoot when everyone you love dies and you keep living?" His voice got quieter. "It won't."

"I'll find someone else to love," Hudson said.

It took a special low for someone to carry a flask around in their robe pocket. Smith reached down and took a sip from the open flask in his damp robe pocket.

"That's cold," he said.

"2004?" Hudson asked again. "What happened when you two went back in time?"

Smith looked at him through bloodshot eyes. "Brooks died. I died. I got better. He didn't."

"That's all?" Hudson wondered.

"I honestly don't remember anything from like 2012 to 2045," Smith said.

Hudson noticed that Smith had included the two years before his disappearance, and judged him. "Thirty three years? You took his death a little too hard, don't you think?"

"What?" Smith responded to the implication that he'd become an overemotional alcoholic with a 'how dare you' glance. "No, it wasn't like that. After the... incident, the Reticent picked me up and kept me locked up for years. I can vaguely recall it being horrible, but it's all gone. Just flashes of light and experiments and..." He recalled a stabbing pain in his chest and froze. *Did they pull my lungs out?* He took another sip from his flask and shook the thought off. "I just want it to be over. I tried going back and killing my past self, but that didn't stick, so I keep using the machine and getting a little bit older. It doesn't always work, but—"

Hudson interrupted. "It doesn't always work?"

"No? Is that a problem for you?" Smith asked.

A lack of inquisitiveness was always a problem for Hudson. "Did you ever stop to think about why that might be? Did you ever stop to think about it at all?"

"Hey," warned Smith. "I looked for you and you were nowhere to be found." He paused. "Do you think there's a problem?"

"With the aging thing? No, not really," Hudson admitted. "I wish you were really future me, though."

"Well, I wish you were future you too," Smith said.

Hudson considered that. "Maybe we can help each other out..."

23 / TIME ISN'T ON MY SIDE

Back in 2011, Arturo Brooks cried. Not the larger-than-life wail of someone who had just watched his entire family's deaths at the hands of wraiths, but the soft sobbing of someone who'd just had his heart broken.

In spite of its salacious beginnings, the relationship between him and Smith had turned out to be a good one. At least Brooks thought so. Smith, on the other hand, having noticed that his reflection had begun to resemble the traumatized self he'd seen years earlier, decided that it was time to end it. He broke the news at bedtime, which is the second worst time to break news after 'during a plane crash.'

"I don't understand," Brooks said. He sat on the edge of the bed next to his partner, dejected.

"I..." Smith didn't have a good explanation. "I don't have a good explanation. I just know this isn't going to work out." He wasn't lying, but it didn't make a very compelling breakup speech.

Brooks was appropriately insulted. "What kind of... if you don't love me, just say so. What you just said is dumb."

Smith hyperfocused on that phrase. *If you don't love me.* He grabbed the sides of his partner's face and stared into his eyes. "Don't ever think that."

"What?" Brooks sniffed.

"I never loved anyone before you. Not my parents. Definitely not my real parents. Not one person I ever fucked. Just you... and I need you to know that."

It was one of the more romantic uses of the word 'fuck' in history. He continued gazing into Brooks's eyes. Even soaked with tears, they were beautiful. He pulled the younger man in for what was intended to be one last, short kiss. Their tears, which had run down each man's face and onto his lips, mingled. But the kiss wasn't short. Every time Smith began to pull away, Brooks pulled him in.

Finally, Smith choked out a "Stop it."

"I don't know what's wrong," Brooks said, "but whatever it is, we can beat it."

Smith wanted to say "you can't beat time," but he couldn't, so he settled for a simple, gloomy "We can't."

This breakup sucked. The amount Smith had grown to care for his partner over four years was previously unheard of for him. How much he would love Brooks in a few more years—that was terrifying. And it was getting closer and closer to that time. It had to end, for self-preservation's sake.

"I don't care," said Brooks. "I know you won't tell me until you're ready, but I don't care. Whatever it is—"

It had to end, but Smith lacked the resolve to end it. Brooks was as dedicated to him as he was to Brooks, and the look on his face—that stupidly determined, beautiful look—rendered him unable to finish the job he'd set out to.

"It's serious," Smith said, trying to simultaneously explain himself and avoid explaining himself as he moved to wipe a tear from his eye.

Brooks beat him to it, and his hand lingered on the side of his partner's face. "Eddie... we've got this."

Goddamnit, Smith thought.

The feeling of certain doom that filled him in that moment would stick with him for quite some time.

In 2090, the same feeling was stuck with Smith as he stared into his bathroom mirror. 'Certain doom' was a strange feeling for someone who could never experience doom. It was especially strange for someone who desperately wanted to.

I'm really fucked up, he thought.

After he changed out of his dragon-revealing bathrobe and

into his everyday clothing (an old t-shirt and depression sweatpants), Smith sat with Patience and Hudson in the dining room. He made coffee for the lot of them, uncapping a bottle of bourbon so that his own was Irish. 2090's Edward Smith was a profoundly unhappy man who had no recourse but liquor, and lots of it. He'd fully embraced the drunk detective lifestyle that had formerly been a front, and while he was still as blunt and crass as ever, he'd lost the spark that kept him from ending it all back in the early 2000s.

"You really want to die?" Hudson asked.

"I do," Smith said, offering no further explanation.

"Well, you may get your wish," Hudson said. "You remember the rift over Manhattan? The first time around, in 2014?"

Smith shook his head. "Barely? I told you—"

"Yeah, blackout. Got it."

Smith glowered. "That's not what I said—"

Hudson set his coffee down as if to prepare himself for his own bad news. "When we arrived here, the rift was back. You're the one who came to the past and told everyone time was collapsing, right? Pretending to be me?"

"Yeah, why?"

Hudson made the facial expression equivalent of '...' and asked, "You want to explain what the hell that was about?"

"I don't know, man. You told me to do it."

Hudson sought clarification. "Future me told you to go back and tell past you and Brooks to go see me?"

"Yeah, he called a while back," Smith said. He added, "I need a drink."

"But you have a drink," Patience noted.

"Did he—uh—I explain why?" Hudson asked. He couldn't figure out why he wouldn't just take care of things himself, unless he couldn't. Was future him in trouble?

"Yeah, he explained," Smith said. " There really was some kind of anomaly started in 2014. Something something physics, you know, and now it's spreading throughout time or whatever."

"Why didn't I just go myself?" Hudson wondered. "I could have explained everything."

"I don't know. Ask yourself. Oh... that's right. *You're not here*," Smith sneered.

"Were you planning on doing anything about this? Doing some detective work maybe? Isn't that what you do?"

"No?" Smith shrugged. "Did you miss the part where I'm trying to die?"

"Your own personal death wish is a little different from sentencing the entire universe to collapse," said Hudson.

"It's not like I'm *causing* it," Smith said. "I just don't care if it happens. It'll be easier than trying to age myself through time travel, I'll tell you that."

If there was one thing Hudson Marrow couldn't tolerate, it was lactose. If there was one other thing he couldn't tolerate, it was nihilism. He'd had some rough times—who hadn't?—but there was always something worth looking forward to. A new discovery. A new relationship. A new Star Wars movie (if only he'd known what became of the series after Episode XXI). That Smith was only 114 years old and ready to call it quits was simply unacceptable. Something inside him overcame his desire to remain mild-mannered, and he slapped Smith in the side of the face.

"What the hell?" Smith complained.

Patience gasped.

"We're going to figure this out, and we're going to save the world," Hudson said.

Smith corrected him. "You are. I'm gonna stay here and get drunk and hope you fail." He strolled across the room and plopped into a lounge chair.

Hudson let out an exasperated sigh. "Jesus Christ."

Patience gasped again.

"Come on," Hudson said, grabbing Smith by the hand in

an attempt to drag him out of the chair toward the door.

Smith planted himself in the chair. "I told you no."

Hudson let go and folded his arms. "Let me show you something. You're going to want to see this."

"Unless it's the inevitable heat death of the universe, I doubt it." Smith chugged the last of his coffee, then stood. "Where are we going?

"To see your partner," Hudson said.

Smith felt fire under his face. He hadn't fought in years, but he violently shoved Hudson away. "You're not funny. You're not clever. You're not taking me to a cemetery so I can see a gravestone and get inspired or whatever. He's dead."

"I have a time machine."

"Do you think I haven't tried?" Smith asked, his voice desperate. "I've gone back and tried to stop him from trying to save his family. I've gone back and tried to kill my past self. I've gone back and left letters to myself so maybe past me would figure it out. At one point there were, like, six of me on the scene in 2004, including one I'm pretty sure was a mirror universe version because I'd never sport a goatee. We all failed."

"Just because you can't save him doesn't mean we can't visit him," Hudson noted.

"Yeah? I think Brooksy would have told me if he'd ever encountered my future self gallivanting around in a time machine with a dick scientist and a pilgrim."

"Actually," Hudson corrected, "she's a Puritan."

"Why does anybody know or care what the difference is? Oh my nonexistent God."

Patience gasped.

"Shut up and come with me," Hudson said.

After a brief, defiant moment, Smith ran out of resolve and allowed the physicist to drag him toward the door.

24 / A JUMP TO THE LEFT

The very out of shape Smith was not easy to drag outside, but he had so little will to resist that it made the job easier. Hudson pulled him toward the gate where he'd left the time machine, and Patience, unsure of what to do other than dutifully follow, dutifully followed the pair.

That's when things got really, really weird. In addition to Hudson Marrow circa 2014 and Hudson Marrow circa 2090, who was really Edward Smith, a third Hudson Marrow, who called himself Stan Sanford, stood beside his own time machine, which had parked next to Hudson's. He offered a friendly wave. Smith looked from Hudson to Stan, then down at himself.

"You know," Smith said. "This is why people don't write time travel stories."

Hudson was a big fan of science fiction and disputed that claim. "That's not true. H.G. Wells did it and he was a master."

"Well, I bet he thought it was a master pain in the ass."

"We could ask him," Stan said, half serious.

Patience had no idea what they were talking about.

Accompanying Stan were Tangelo and Lemon Jones, siblings from the moon. This adventure was their first journey through time, but more importantly for Lemon, it was her first journey to Earth. And now that they weren't in 1690s Salem, she could explore. She'd read about the planet—certainly more than is healthy—and considered herself a history buff, but actually seeing Earth in 2090 blew her mind.

"Are those—?" she asked, looking at the imperfectly tailored landscaping.

"More trees, yes," Stan said.

Patience quietly wondered what sort of creature could be

overwhelmed by trees. They were, after all, practically the only thing she'd seen for the first fifteen years of her life. She thought it might have had something to do with their being dark-skinned, but—luckily for her—she didn't express that view.

Stan sought to confirm the identities of the people in front of him. "Hudson Marrow? Patience Cloyce?"

They nodded.

Smith griped. "It's about time you came back, you dick."

"Oh, that?" Stan avoided eye contact. "I didn't. I remained in Texas and continued my research. I'm from the year 2202. This is my personal aide, Tangelo Jones, and his sister, Lemon."

"And I thought kids today had stupid names," Smith said.

"Our parents owned a citrus farm," Tangelo said, defending his fruity name.

"Yeah? My parents ran a meth lab," Smith said. "They didn't name me Ephedrine."

"Why are you here?" Hudson asked his future self.

Stan responded with a question of his own. "You've all seen the rift, right?"

Everyone nodded. It was hard to miss.

"Well I was looking out at Earth last night and it disappeared," Stan said.

"Yeah, it keeps appearing and disappearing on and off," Hudson said.

"No. *Earth* disappeared," corrected Stan.

That took everyone a long time to process. Questions started firing from all over the place.

"Where were you looking at Earth from?" Hudson asked.

"Luna."

"What do you mean it disappeared?" Smith asked.

"The entire thing was replaced by the empty void. There was nothing there. Then, without Earth's gravitational pull, Luna began to experience an event," Stan said.

"What kind of event?" Hudson asked.

"It was destroyed," said Stan. "I grabbed my assistant and escaped in my time machine."

Smith's anger was audible. "You had me replace you, went to the goddamn moon, and never contacted me again?"

"Yes," Stan answered matter-of-factly.

Hudson grabbed Smith from behind and stopped him from lunging at his future self.

"Do you know how miserable I've been?" Smith asked.

"How?" Stan gestured toward his house. "I gave you all this."

"You gave me a giant pile of bullshit." Smith shook himself free and took off, muttering to himself. He was going to go back inside, get his things, and get the hell out of Stan-Hudson's house.

Stan sighed.

"Do we really need that guy?" Tangelo asked.

"He has something to do with the source of the anomaly back in 2014," Hudson said.

"So... you want to go after him?" Stan asked.

Patience interrupted. "Sirs?"

Neither man knew how to respond.

"I don't think Mr. Smith likes either of you very much. I could go speak with him," she said.

It seemed a sure bet that the Puritan from 1692 wouldn't be able to draw Smith out, but it was worth a try.

"Tangelo, will you go with her?" Stan asked.

His aide nodded. Stan handed Tangelo a tranquilizer and whispered exactly what he should do with it when (not if) Smith decided to be noncompliant. His aide nodded again.

Lemon followed her brother, for the drama. It was set to be far juicier than whatever conversation Hudson and Stan would have about quantum physics.

Upstairs, Smith packed a small duffel bag to the brim with clothes and booze. As he rifled through his things, it occurred to him that something was missing. He began pulling drawers out of their slots and cursing his organizational skills in the same way that he cursed most things.

Patience and the Jones siblings approached cautiously, not wanting to get hit by any airborne shoes.

"Sir?" Patience asked. She then cursed herself for again forgetting her instruction not to say "sir."

Smith was halfway through the phrase "I told you I don't give a shit" when he realized it wasn't Hudson or Hudson-turned-Stan who had come to pester him. He changed his sentiment, ever so slightly. "I don't know why they sent three kids up here, but I don't need a pep talk." He continued throwing shirts out into the open.

"I'm immortal too, si... Mr. Smith."

"Yeah. Congratulations." With the last drawer emptied, Smith maneuvered his way over to the closet and began pillaging the items there. He paused briefly over a charred copy of the board game LIFE, then tossed it aside in search of his item.

Patience continued speaking. "If I understand correctly, that means I will never die."

Smith rolled his eyes. "Yeah, that's what immortal means."

"Then it seems to me that I should befriend others who share my situation," Patience said.

That was the most sensible thing Smith had heard all day, and his mind immediately rebelled against it. "Just because we're both immortal doesn't mean we have anything in common."

"Actually—" Tangelo started.

"Shut up." Smith turned to Patience. "*You* are a fifteen-year-old pilgrim from 16-whatever. I'm a bisexual alcoholic from four hundred years in your future. You don't even know what the words 'alcoholic' and 'bisexual' mean. If you want yourself an eternal friend, look somewhere else."

"I don't know where else to look," she pleaded. "Mr.

Brooks was kind, and—"

Just as she said the name, Smith found exactly what he'd been looking for: a well-worn corrugated cardboard box, approximately twelve-by-eight inches and five inches deep. That box contained everything he could scavenge from the Brooks/Smith brownstone after it was cleared by Reticent agents—everything aside from the game of LIFE. Smith ignored the teenagers that surrounded him and, sitting cross-legged on the floor, opened it.

Nothing in the box was particularly important. Eighty years earlier, Smith wouldn't have given any of it a second glance. Now, though, it was the most important box in the world, and it had to come with him, wherever he was going. The first thing he saw inside was the crappy Ralex watch he bought from a street vendor when he first moved to the city. Brooks always gave him shit about that watch and the sentimentality it demonstrated.

Then there was a copy of *To Kill a Mockingbird*, Brooks's favorite book. Smith always gave him shit about that book. As soon as he was freed from Reticent captivity, though, he read it six times, poring over every word, trying to figure out what it was his late partner loved so much about it. He never did.

The kids huddled over his shoulder, and Patience tried to get his attention. "Mr. Smith?"

"You okay, mister?" Lemon added.

Smith might as well have been alone. He ignored them and handled the items in the box one by one. That stupid copy of LL Cool J's *All World 2*. Brooks knew how much he hated LL Cool J and thought it would be a funny birthday gift. On December 4, 2010, it was. He considered the fact that LL Cool J had not one but two greatest hits albums and decided once again that the world was not just. Of course, he didn't need LL to come to that conclusion. All these reminders that Arturo Brooks was dead were enough. Smith picked up one last memento: a picture of the two at a Reticent holiday party. It was probably the only photo they'd ever taken in which Smith had a smile on his face. The two men stood, arms around each other in a way that could have conceivably been platonic, drinks in their other hands, having a great time. They were fresh off the Goblin King victory, and life couldn't have been any better. Even with Smith holding back because he knew the future, they always had a great time. He imagined how much better it would have been without that fear. With that thought, Smith ran his thumb down the left side of the photo and let himself cry.

Patience glanced at the Joneses. They, like her, stood in uncomfortable silence. She looked back down at Smith. She had no idea what photographs were or how they worked, but something about this one caught her eye. She leaned in to get a closer look.

Smith didn't slap her, but he felt like he could have.

"Back off," he said.

"I... know them," she said, eyes fixed on some Reticent agents in the background of the photo. "I know them."

25 / A STEP TO THE RIGHT

In 2012, the same year the picture was taken, agents Brooks and Smith moved in together. As they unpacked dozens of boxes filled with dozens of things neither man really needed, they drank dozens of sips of bourbon. Brooks sat on the floor, perplexed by an IKEA shelf.

"Something's missing," he said, jabbing a wooden peg at a hole where it wouldn't fit.

"Did you try lubing it up first?" Smith asked.

The glare he received could have won the Academy Award for Best Glare. "I'm serious. There's supposed to be a screw or something."

Smith choked back a laugh at his own incoming pun. "Are you saying you're... a screw loose?"

"I hate you," Brooks said drolly.

"You're not the only one," Smith said, shrugging.

That lighthearted jab got dark quickly. Brooks muttered an "oh my God" to himself, chose not to respond, and proceeded to check the parts bag for the fourth time. Confirming that there was, in fact, no screw, Brooks frowned.

"We're gonna have to go back to the store," he said.

"No. Wait." Smith perked up, eyeing the floor near Brooks. "Don't move."

Brooks obliged, and Smith knelt down and picked up a three-inch screw that was wedged into the carpet only a foot from his partner. He picked it up and dramatically waved it in front of his partner's face.

"Is this your card?" he asked.

Brooks clapped his hands together. "I love you."

"You only love me when I screw you," said Smith.

Brooks's face turned to stone. "And we're back to hate."

Brooks reached for the screw and Smith pulled it away,

tutting.

"Not with that attitude," he said.

Brooks groaned. "It's late and I have been assembling this shelf for *two hours*."

"Fiiiine," Smith said with a sigh. He placed the screw in Brooks's hand, then clasped his own around it, tight. With hands locked, he pulled his partner in for a kiss.

When he pulled away, Smith pointed at the shelf and chastised Brooks in a faux transatlantic accent. "Now get back to work. That shelf's not going to build itself, see."

The glare he received this time wouldn't have won the Academy Award for Best Glare, but it would have been nominated and lost to Daniel Day-Lewis. Brooks inserted the screw into the slot and within a few minutes, they had a very exciting Nornäs model bookcase.

"So what do we need this shelf for?" Smith asked.

"Um..." Brooks shuffled his hands about as a distraction while he tried to think of something. He came up empty. "I stayed up until 3AM building this thing and I have no idea what it's for."

There was a brief moment of silence before both men broke into guffaws.

"Holy shit," Smith said.

Brooks slumped. "We *have* to find something to put on this thing."

"We can figure it out in the morning," Smith said.

"No. I didn't spend all this time on a pointless shelf," Brooks insisted. "Open that box over there."

Smith tore open a large box labeled 'Misc.' It lived up to its name, boasting a few hats, a deck of cards, a wall calendar, an artificial bouquet, and the board game LIFE.

"Okay," Smith said. "You give *me* shit about not being organized and *this* is your idea of packing?"

"Just give me something. Anything."

Smith took Brooks's LIFE and handed it to him. Brooks,

in turn, placed it on the top shelf, proudly displaying the game's gauchely colorful labeling.

"There," he said. "It's starting to look like a home, don't you think?"

"Oh, yeah," Smith said. He looked around the living room. "It looks like the weird home of someone who has one piece of furniture and a board game, but—"

"And," Brooks said, interrupting his partner's sarcasm, "it's sort of symbolic."

"Because it's a big gay rainbow?"

Brooks glowered. "No. Because we're starting a *life* together, and that's the first thing that goes up. I like it."

"Yeah..."

Brooks didn't see the pain in his partner's face at that moment.

In the realest sense, the Arturo Brooks of 2014 could see pain. He could see a lot of things human beings aren't supposed to see: temperature, heartbeat, brain activity...

He didn't know what was happening to him. All he knew was that he woke up strapped to a wall feeling ill, at least partly from dreaming about all the awful fates that could have befallen Smith. One moment, Brooks had been gallivanting around the past, trying to stop his family from being murdered. Then there was pain, in his body and in his partner's eyes. Then he was here, trapped in some dark room.

Did someone shoot me?

With his forehead strapped down, he couldn't look down at his arms and legs, but he had a hunch—based on the total lack of sensation below his neck—that he was paralyzed.

When a doctor finally walked into the room and flicked on the light, Brooks's field of vision was flooded by the world's best heads-up display.

The doctor's pulse was apparently 84. His blood pressure was 118/73. His estimated age was 47. Brooks knew this because the information appeared in bold orange Helvetica font right in front of his face. He looked around as best as he could, trying to find the computer to which he was undoubtedly hooked. He saw nothing.

"You're finally awake," the doctor said.

"*Finally?*" Brooks asked. "How long was I out?"

"About a week."

"Where's Eddie?" Brooks asked. The last thing he saw was his partner's face as he lost consciousness back in 2004.

"You sure do dream about your partner a lot," the doctor said. "He's fine."

"Where am I?" Brooks asked.

"I think you already know," said the doctor.

Brooks knew. No group but the Reticent would be interested in attaching him to a wall and performing experiments on him. Working at the Reticent accustomed agents to the idea that they could be dismissed, mindwiped, or killed at any time. As such, most agents had come from rough backgrounds and either didn't see much value in their own lives (see: Smith, Edward) or saw so much value in others that they were hyper-focused on the 'saving the world' aspects of the organization (see: Brooks, Arturo).

"What are you going to do with me?" he asked.

"We're already done," said the doctor. "What do you think we were doing for a week?"

"I died..." Brooks's stomach sank. Nothing had come after, but he knew he had died. Everything about being in Reticent HQ—about being alive—felt wrong.

"Very good. Yes, you did. We brought you back to life in an enhanced cybernetic body. It's the first of its kind. You should be flattered."

"Charmed," Brooks said dryly.

The doctor elaborated. "The experiment is to see how long

you can live. We believe these bodies may be the key to un-locking immortality for all of our agents."

"Why?" Brooks asked.

"Think of how advanced your knowledge is compared to a new recruit. But you're getting older. Your reaction time is down. Your glory days are behind you."

"I'm 32," Brooks said. "*Thanks.*"

"If we can keep you from aging," the doctor said, "the Reticent will have access to your advanced skillset indefinitely."

"You're assuming that I'd want to work for you for eternity," Brooks said.

"*Want* doesn't really come into play here." The doctor stared at Brooks with cold eyes. "Dead men have no agency."

26 / NOT THIS SHIT AGAIN

For a third time, Hudson Marrow held Smith's picture in front of Patience's face. The Puritan girl dutifully squinted her eyes to show that she was making a careful observation.

"Are you sure?" Hudson asked.

For the third time, she nodded. "Yes, sir."

Stan, who'd visited Salem, offered his concurrence.

In the background of the photograph, behind Brooks and Smith, there was a commotion—at least, as much commotion as a corporate holiday party would allow. Among the agents making acceptably wacky poses were William Stoughton of Salem magistrate fame, and John Wilmington, Patience's neighbor-turned-executioner.

"Is *everyone* immortal these days?" Smith asked. He said it in his usual sarcastic manner, but if there was a chance that Brooks had recovered from his death, he genuinely needed to know.

Tangelo raised a hand. "I'm not."

"Me neither," Lemon said. "As far as the blumpkins go."

Stan and Hudson simultaneously put their hands to their chins and pondered. They both considered the immortality thing, but Hudson also tried to derive a non-explicit meaning for blumpkin. He came up blank on that front; it was just a mysterious piece of future slang he'd have to accept.

"How long have you been immortal?" Hudson asked Patience.

"I don't know, sir," she said. "I know that I used to suffer scrapes and bruises, but that being hanged did not kill me. Yesterday I was able to press my wounds together and they were healed immediately."

"When was the last time you were injured before you were hanged?" Stan asked.

Patience thought about that for a moment. "Just before I found the letter addressed to Stan, I scraped my leg against a fallen tree branch."

"And you, Agent Smith?" Hudson asked.

"Not an agent," Smith griped before answering. "I've been injured a thousand times. As far as I know, it changed when I went back in time and got shot in the head. I figure the Reticent revived me and screwed with my genes or something."

"Hmm." Stan had an idea. He took his pocketknife and held it out toward Lemon.

Tangelo took offense to that, and stood in front of his sister, defiant. Lemon rolled her eyes.

"I'm going to check both of you," Stan said.

Before Tangelo could dodge him, Stan slid the blade along the back of his aide's hand. The only thing that happened was Tangelo began bleeding.

He took his jacket off and wrapped the sleeve around his hand. "What did you do that for? I already told you I'm not immortal."

"Just wait," Stan said.

He repeated the procedure on Lemon. To everyone's surprise but his own, her wound began healing itself.

Lemon's eyes grew wide. "What just happened?"

"What did you take from my office?" Stan countered.

She dodged an awful stare from her brother and pulled a spirograph out of her backpack. "Sorry, but it seemed like the whole place was gonna be destroyed and this thing—"

"You recognize that?" Stan asked his past self.

Hudson nodded. "I, uh... we went back and picked it up in 1974." What his future self was suggesting dawned on him suddenly and he turned to Smith. "You stole my lighter."

"God, are you still mad about that?" Smith asked.

Patience gasped.

"I had that lighter in my pocket when I traveled back to

Mesopotamia," Hudson said. He understood.

Smith did not. "*So?*"

Stan addressed the entire group. "I... we," he said gesturing to Hudson, "were born this way. Our parents raised us knowing we healed from every cut, every scrape, and every bruise. I've, uh... *we've* traveled back and tried to find an explanation for it, but there isn't any. Our mother wasn't special. Our biological father wasn't special. He was a Schwan's delivery truck driver. We're just different. None of you were born immortal. You picked it up, and I think I know where from."

The scientists hypothesized that some sort of energy transference had transpired. Perhaps, when an object went through time with an immortal person, that object could absorb their immortality and grant it to someone else. That could explain why Smith aged as a result of constantly using the machine. More importantly, it raised the question of who else that immortality had been transferred to.

"How many suicide notes did you say you left in the past?" Hudson asked.

"I didn't say they were *suicide notes*," Smith said.

Hudson shot him a pointed look.

"Few dozen, maybe," said Smith.

"And what happened to the letter you found?" Hudson asked Patience.

"It was sentenced to burn, sir."

"Did you see it burn?" Hudson asked.

"No, sir. I was being hanged at the time."

Stan shook his head. "I think we know what happened to those other Puritans then."

"What are you gonna do about it?" Smith asked. "Go back and take the letters away from them?"

"That's not how this works," Stan said. "They already got their hands on the letters, so whatever we did or didn't do had that end result. I just wonder... how many immortals did we create?" While he preferred immortality, he didn't care much for the notion of inflicting it on people without their consent. Smith was a perfect enough example of why that was no good.

Hudson perked up, remembering the apartment full of immortality-granting artifacts he'd left on Staten Island.

"I need to get back home," he said.

"Hold on," said Stan. "We haven't figured out what's happening with this rift."

Hudson was already half inside his time machine when he turned and replied. "Maybe this has something to do with it. Maybe people aren't meant to be immortal. All we know is that it started in 2014 and that's where I'm going. Come on."

Smith found himself torn between his deathwish and his affinity for investigation. There was something admittedly intriguing about members of the Reticent being 300-year-old pilgrims. If there was some connection between them and the rift, he would rather be the one to discover it than not be the one to discover it. Besides, discovering it wouldn't necessarily mean he had to stop it. All things considered, he could hasten his death—maybe by leaping into the thing. He picked up his bag and agreed to return to the past.

Hudson's time machine was too small to carry six people. Luckily, there were two: the one Hudson and Patience had used to go from 2014 to 2090, and the one in which Stan and the Joneses made their journey from 2202 to 1694 and back to 2090. Everyone returned to the machine from which they'd come.

Smith crammed in next to Patience—his 2090 form taking a lot more space than she remembered—and they were off.

27 / IN THE BEDROOM

The first time machine landed back where it came from: in Hudson Marrow's bedroom. Smith was the first to stumble out and he immediately puked on Hudson's duvet cover.

"Do you have to get fluids on my bed every time you're here?" Hudson asked.

Smith would have laughed, but he didn't remember what the scientist was talking about and Hudson's joke fell flat. Just another pitfall of time travel.

All three passengers were struck by the fact that there was noise coming from the other room. No one else lived with Hudson Marrow. No one else could tolerate living with Hudson Marrow, which involved having to search beneath piles of dirty clothing just to find a fork, then realizing that there was nothing to eat with said fork.

There was a loud crash, and Hudson and Smith scurried to the best of their abilities to confront its source.

In the living room, a middle-aged man held the Aztec feather shield, practicing his defensive stance.

"Who are you and what are you doing in my living room?" Hudson demanded.

"Relax. I'm just taking this outside to get a price."

Hudson gesticulated. "You're WHAT?"

"Yeah, it's fine," said a low female voice.

Hudson recognized it as that of Meena, Veronica's best friend. The woman was tucked in behind a room divider, keeping an eye on the apartment's items. Half the things in the room now bore round purple stickers.

The man took the shield and hurried off.

"What's going on?" Hudson asked.

"Yard sale," Meena answered.

"You have a yard?" Smith asked.

"No." Hudson turned to Meena and repeated the word more loudly. "NO."

"Everything with a purple sticker is for sale," she said.

"I haven't been gone more than a day." He threw up his hands. "You have no right to sell my things!"

"I don't, no. But anything you buy while you're married is community property, sooo..."

Hudson cursed to himself. "Veronica."

Sure enough, when he rushed over to the window and looked down on the complex's green, he saw six tables lined up and covered in artifacts. Even the marble slab hadn't been safe, and now glistened in the sunlight, a beacon for bargain shoppers. Sitting amidst the chaos was Veronica Marrow, currently receiving one hundred dollars for a priceless Aztec feather shield.

"Can you take care of her?" Hudson asked Smith.

Smith wasn't sure whether Hudson meant Patience or Meena, but it didn't matter. He took care of Meena by escorting her to the door and promptly shoving her out. He took care of Patience by insisting that she take a seat and watch television. She obliged, as she was wont to do. The program was, unfortunately, the evening news, and Smith soon found himself subjected to a story about Canadian popstar Justin Bieber accidentally flashing some paparazzi.

"Who is Justin Bieber?" Patience asked.

"It doesn't matter," Smith said.

The next story was about a panda birth at the Beijing Zoo. Smith rolled his eyes.

The next story was a human-interest piece about some legless tennis player. Smith remained unmoved.

The next story caught his attention. A brownstone fire on Decatur Street in Brooklyn had claimed half a block of homes. That couldn't have been a coincidence, but why would the Reticent bother erasing the lives of two agents who had no family to miss them? That sort of treatment was normally reserved for when they were trying to send a message.

Smith perked up. If the 2014 version of him was currently stuck in Reticent headquarters being tortured, then who could they be sending a message to other than Brooks? He rubbed at a cramp in his abdomen. For the first time in decades, he felt something close to hope, and his body didn't like it.

He quickly brought himself back to reality. The Reticent were probably just clearing evidence and someone got a little overzealous with the gasoline. At best, they were sending a message to other agents: break the rules and we'll erase everything about you. Still, there was some nagging hope inside him and it was not appreciated.

The next story, finally, was about the enormous rift over Manhattan. A peppy female news anchor explained. "Experts remain puzzled by the cloud over Manhattan—"

"A *cloud?*" Smith muttered.

"—News Team 8 will let you know when we have more information." She quickly transitioned to the next story: a U.S. Senator had made a huge gaffe by referring to the internet as "the worldwide web."

Smith threw his hands up in frustration.

Outside, Hudson gestured madly at Veronica as he approached his estranged wife counting the significant stack of cash she had collected that morning. In front of her were an impressive number of records and receipts for a yard sale started with one day's notice.

"What do you think you're doing?" he asked.

"Selling some of my extra stuff," she smirked.

"It's not *your* stuff!"

"Half of everything, baby."

She handed him half the money in her hands and Hudson sighed. He turned to the man packing a feather shield into the back of his nondescript SUV.

"Hey!" he shouted. "You can't have that!"

"'Scuse me?" the man replied as Hudson confronted him.

Hudson sorted $100 and shoved it at him. "No sale. Take your money."

The man brushed the hand away. "Too late, pal."

Hudson was dumbstruck. "What? Too late? How is it—"

He turned to Veronica, who simply shrugged. Hudson responded to that sentiment with a series of frantic gestures and mouthing the words "damn it" repeatedly. As Hudson objected to the situation, the man hopped into his driver's seat and sped off, feather shield in tow.

"It's not your stuff," Hudson repeated, head in hands.

Veronica rolled her eyes. "Oh, you can go buy more."

"I didn't get to finish," Hudson said. "It's not your stuff, and it's not my stuff."

"Come again?"

"We need to talk."

28 / WHOOPS

As the other time machine spun slowly to a halt, one of its occupants raised a fair question.

"What are we looking for?" Tangelo asked.

"Agent Smith," Stan said.

The Smith from 2090 had forgotten over thirty years of his eternal life, and that thirty years just happened to coincide with the appearance of an enormous, universe-consuming rift? There were coincidences, certainly, but that didn't seem like a coincidence. Not when Smith worked for a shady organization full of immortal Puritans who just happened to come from the same town as a girl who appeared at exactly the same time as the rift. No, this was not a coincidence.

Tangelo didn't think so either. "I know *who* we're looking for. I mean, what's this place look like?"

Having parked the time machine behind a nearby bush, the group stood on the corner directly across from Reticent headquarters. The building looked like it would house a bed and breakfast or a new age medicine shop. It was stone, with tasteful purple awnings over the windows. It wasn't the kind of building that should be used by a group that called itself the Reticent. On the other hand, it was the exact kind of building that a reticent group would use.

"It looks like that, from what I remember," Stan said.

It had been centuries, and he wasn't completely sure, as there were no agents swarming the premises this time. "We can't use the time machine to get in. There's some sort of barrier around the building."*

"So what are we gonna do?" Lemon asked.

"You," her brother answered, "are gonna stay in the

---

* It was pixie plasma, sourced from the sixth dimension.

machine and wait for us to get out." He gestured toward the bush.

"Why? I can help," she insisted.

Tangelo dismissed her. "You're seventeen."

She pointed out an inconvenient fact. "You were seventeen when mom and dad died."

Stan pretended he was doing something with his phone and shied away from the teenagers while he scoped out the building.

"The whole point," Tangelo said, "is for you to not have to grow up as fast as I did."

"I *am* grown up," she whined.

Lemon had always had what some refer to as an "old soul." Grownups were interesting, unlike members of her own age group. She wished she had been a teenager in the early 2000s. People who grew up in the Great Recession, she thought, knew what was *really* important. She couldn't define exactly what those things were, but she maintained with great certainty that people two hundred years earlier were better.

"You're not coming," Tangelo said. "Period."

Lemon sourly bit her tongue as her brother escorted her back into the machine. When Stan and Tangelo began discussing their plans and she was unable to hear them from her seat, she scowled. When the two men navigated to the front door of Reticent headquarters and went inside, she jumped out of the time machine and hurried off. If she wasn't going to be part of the mission, she was at least going to soak up some history. And there was no better time to do so, what with all the tourists having gone home on account of the giant rift, and most residents having stayed inside on account of the same.

Her hipster instincts led her to a nearby subway station.

*
**

To the outside world, the Reticent was a normal medical research firm. There were even tours of the upper floors available every Tuesday and Thursday from 8-10AM. Inside the building, Stan and Tangelo pushed their way through a tour group and stopped at the Information desk.

"Can I help you?" the woman behind it asked, looking up from filing her nails.

Stan responded honestly. "Hi. Yes. I'm a time traveler from the year 2202. I need to speak with Agent Edward Smith. It's fairly urgent."

She glanced at her monitor, where a blistery purple monster nodded; the Dror detected no lies in Stan's statement. The disinterest on the woman's face showed that this was not the strangest request she'd heard this week. It was, however, a Code Fourteen, which meant it was going to take significantly more effort (and more paperwork) than any other requests. She phoned Charlotte Nguyen's extension. There was no answer.

"Oh, that's right," she said.

Stan and Tangelo shared a puzzled look.

She corrected her error and phoned Travis Marsh's extension. Following Nguyen's erasure, her position was given to a 5'3" ex-cop with a serious problem. Not a drinking problem or a problem with corruption or something else typical to ex-cops in fiction. This was a real problem. He'd never worked with either Brooks or Smith, but he was now in charge of their cases. If (read: when) the two men caused another spectacular disaster, it was his existence that would be on the line.

The speakerphone allowed Stan and Tangelo to hear him answer with a growl. "Travis Marsh."

"I have a Code Fourteen here to speak to you about Agent Smith," she said.

Marsh hung up the phone, but it didn't save him from the situation. Twenty minutes and three calls later, two men from the future stood in his doorway asking to speak with his rogue agent.

"Agent Smith is indisposed," Marsh said. "You're going to have to work with me."

"We can't really do that," Stan said. He approached and shook Marsh's damp hand. "Stan Sanford. President of Luna, 2202. This is my assistant, Tangelo Jones."

Tangelo leaned in and followed with a handshake of his own. "Pleasure meeting you."

"Travis Marsh," the man repeated through heavy breathing. "Can you at least explain why you need to speak with Agent Smith and not anyone else?"

"I really have to insist that we see Agent Smith. The universe hangs in the balance," Stan said.

"Can you prove you're from the future?" Marsh asked.

Stan thought about it for a moment, then offered a suggestion. "I can show you my ID."

By this point, Marsh's sweat had left four visible patches on his shirt: one under each armpit, one in the folds of his stomach, and one perplexing spot atop his left shoulder. If he handled this situation incorrectly, he was worse than dead. What was the correct way to handle it? He couldn't ignore the possibility of destroying the universe. He hadn't failed to notice the rift over the city. Something terrible was happening and there was a chance that he was on the front lines of it. If, on the other hand, he allowed these men to speak with an agent who was being held in isolation and it turned out *not* to be apocalyptic in importance, he was worse than worse than dead. He somehow managed to think hard enough to develop a third option: he could call Agatha Werewith and make sure he didn't displease her.

"Hang on a second," Marsh said.

He dialed the extension, hand shaking. Stan and Tangelo

only heard one end of the conversation, but they could tell exactly how it played out.

"I'm sorry to bother you," Marsh said. A pause. "Yes, of course it's of the utmost importance." Another pause. "I... I *can* handle my own work... It's not that." An extended pause. "I'm so sorry. No... that won't be necessary." A pause. "I apologize again. I'll take care of it."

By this point, Marsh had soaked through his oversized, undertucked button-down. He briefly contemplated fleeing to the Caribbean, but he knew the Reticent would find him wherever he chose to hide and, besides, it was far too hot there for someone with sweating problems.

"Are you okay?" Tangelo asked.

"I have to make the right move," the agent said. "I have to..." Marsh practically begged the men for help. "Show me something convincing... so I have no choice but to help you."

Stan thought about that for a moment. "How about if I tell you that I know about Agents Smith and Brooks."

"Everyone knows about them," Marsh said. "We ignore it because they're good at what they do..."

Stan blinked. "Not that. I know they're both in this building. You just found out Agent Smith is immortal and are currently running experiments on him. As for Agent Brooks, I know he's alive too, and I know what you did to him."

That was good enough for Marsh. Within minutes, the three men were on their way to the twenty-sixth subfloor.

29 / MEANWHILE, ON STATEN ISLAND

Veronica Marrow stood behind the tupperware container that had been acting as a cash drawer, arms crossed and staring at her estranged husband. What he had just said made no sense, and she repeated it for confirmation.

"You invented a time machine?"

Hudson nodded.

"So that's how you do it, huh? That's how you stop aging. You sent your past self here and—"

He interrupted that notion with the truth. "No."

Her eyes struggled to not roll out of her head. "How then?"

"I was born immortal, and thanks to you... you and who knows how many other people probably are too."

She didn't follow, and her expression let him know.

"I'm not sure how it works yet, but if I use the time machine while carrying objects, my immortality sort of... rubs off on them. Sometimes. I guess." Hudson lacked confidence in the theory, but he continued. "I've already made at least one person immortal, and he's not happy about it."

Veronica was silent for a moment, and Hudson was certain he was going to receive an earful about how arrogant he was, how overconfident in his abilities, how childish...

Instead, she literally jumped for joy. "Hudson!"

He stared at her. "What?"

"You don't get it? You've just discovered the Fountain of Youth! That's worth more than any feather shield. Do you know how much people would pay for—"

He threw his hands up and shook his head. "No, no. I can't make this public."

"Why not?" she asked.

"First of all, it seems it's going to age *me*. Second, think about what would happen to the world if everyone on Earth were immortal. Think about the overcrowding. Think about the poverty. Think about how we decide who gets it and who doesn't. Someone gets left behind."

She knew exactly how to make an appeal. "Think about the *knowledge*, Hudson."

He had thought about the knowledge. If human beings, in their short lifespans, could come up with computers, eradicate polio, travel to the moon... there was so much they could do if they only had more time.

A notion gripped his mind. His future self was from the moon. That meant people were going to be living off-planet in just two hundred years. That, he reasoned, couldn't have been coincidental. The space program was in shambles. Private space travel was literally just getting off the ground. What necessitated the move to Luna? What if it was him? What if he had granted immortality to others and marched humanity forward? He tried to talk himself down. If immortality were a common thing in the future, Tangelo and Lemon wouldn't have been surprised when she gained it. Then again, they hadn't acted that terribly surprised, and he *was* fabulously wealthy in the future. People knew he was immortal. Maybe they knew more than that. Someone who had given the world the Fountain of Youth would certainly be famous... His head began to hurt.

While these thoughts were occurring, Hudson stood still, lost in them. Veronica waved a hand in front of his face to bring him back to reality. "Hey, hello?"

"I think you're right," he said. He needed to talk to his future self about this before he made all but one hasty decision. "If I put this out there, you have to do something for me."

"What?" she asked.

"Stay with me," he said, eyes wide and pitiable. "If you're not immortal yet, I can make sure you are and we won't have to worry about you aging—"

That was, without a doubt, the wrong thing to say.

"Are you kidding me? That's pathetic." She continued rebuking him. "You think you're entitled to me because you lucked into being born special? You and I were falling apart well before I started aging and you didn't. Remember Texas?"

He nodded.

"Some things aren't meant to last," she said.

"Like the human lifespan," Hudson pointed out.

Veronica hated that. "If I'd known 'til death do us part' literally meant nothing to you, I never would have gone through with it in the first place."

He corrected her. "No, no. It meant even more to me."

She huffed. "Oh, yeah. It meant a lot. You sleeping with half your students showed me that."

"But think about this: when we got married, I knew I would have to watch you age and die. I knew that I would survive and have that in my memory forever. And I still did it. I knew it would be painful and I still did it." He took her hands and pleaded again. "Please."

"No." She shook her head. "We agreed to end this for the right reasons. Help me live forever or don't, but it has no bearing on our marriage. That's over."

Hudson was crushed, but not so much that he didn't immediately begin scheming.

30 / OBJECT ORIENTED

Arturo Brooks was being programmed. With each passing minute, some memory of who he had been faded, replaced by Reticent codes and orders. And he was conscious of this. If he tried hard enough, he thought, he could keep his memories with him. There was the time he convinced Smith to go on a picnic. It rained and the whole thing was a disaster, but for some reason it made him happy. He couldn't remember why it made him happy—something about a car? There were missing keys and a piece of cake and it might have been in New Hampshire... or New Jersey... or New Mexico...

There are four states with the word 'New' in their names, he thought. It repeats more than any other word. The closest after it are 'North' and 'South.' But the cake...

His attempts at focusing on specific memories were futile; those memories were instantly erased. There had never been and never would be a picnic. The backseat cake shenanigans were gone. In their place were instructions for how to handle a Code Fifteen without handing part of the world over to demons. In the place of feelings were facts. He could, for instance, immediately recall how many states' names began with the word 'New' instead of having to sing the states' names as a song to himself to figure it out.

Brooks wanted to scream but, like his limbs, his mouth was under the control of the agent sitting with a laptop across the room. So long as his brain was connected via a precariously placed USB cable, he belonged to this man. He hated that thought. So long as there was any piece of him left, the only man he belonged to was Smith.

There was a problem, though. He could no longer remember exactly what Smith looked like. He thought he was blond, and maybe his eyes were blue. He wasn't sure.

As the last vestiges of his partner were about to be erased, the door shot open. As it did, Brooks and the scientist were joined by Stan, Tangelo, and Marsh.

"Shut it down," Marsh said. "This is a Code Fourteen and these men need to speak to Agent Smith."

The scientist and Stan shared an incredulous glance. The latter was the one to break the news to Marsh.

"That's not Agent Smith," he said. "That's Agent Brooks."

"Oh, shit," Marsh said. It was only his second day on the job, and it was probably his last.

31 / I'VE BEEN HERE FOR YEARS

In 2013, Brooks felt like his head was going to launch from his neck. Everything in the room was vibrating. It hadn't been a good year for Smith, and his music habits let everyone around him know it. Brooks furiously rubbed his temples, then took a swig of artisanal gin. This was, without a doubt, the worst song he'd ever heard. That he was hearing it upstairs in the bedroom when it was being played two floors down in Smith's office only made it worse. He tried very hard not to interrupt when Smith was in one of these moods, but he was out of migraine pills and the gin wasn't helping, so he made his way downstairs.

The noise—and that's all it was—only got louder. Screeching guitars that made no attempt to resemble chords in their output, fast drumming that seemed about as enjoyable as a child bashing its fists on the next table over at a restaurant, and a voice that was surely choking on something greeted Brooks as he opened the door.

"Can you turn that down, please?"

Smith didn't hear him. It was remarkable that he could still hear at all. He remained in his desk chair, flipping through some case file or another. Brooks walked over to the desk, grabbed the stereo remote, and hit mute. That's when Smith realized he was there.

"I don't touch your music," Smith said, looking up.

"That's not music. I think that's actually banned by the Geneva Convention."

"That was Butterfly Carcass," Smith casually replied.

Brooks shook his head in disbelief. "Butterfly Carcass?"

"Yeah." Smith didn't see what was so strange about that.

"Are you trying to become a parody of yourself, or—"

"Hey, I don't say anything when you're listening to *musica urbana,*" Smith said.

"I hope that's because you recognize it's real music."

"And Butterfly Carcass isn't?"

"No." Brooks remained stone-faced. "I love you, but no." He slid in next to Smith. "What are you researching, anyway?"

He started to lean his head toward his partner's laptop screen, and Smith immediately closed it.

"Nothing," Smith said.

"*Madre de dios*, you're cheating on me," Brooks laughed. "Seriously, you've been holed up in here for days. You working a case without me?"

"Personal project," Smith said. He leaned back in his chair and crossed his arms. "Let's just leave it at that."

As a detective, Brooks was fundamentally incapable of leaving it at that. "Look, whatever the deal is, it'll be easier if we solve it together. You know that, right?"

Smith's answer was a slight, scoffy grunt.

"How many times do we have to do this?" Brooks asked. "You're not alone, and you don't have to act like you are."

"I will be," Smith mumbled to himself.

"Excuse me?" Brooks thought he had heard those words but they weren't completely clear.

"Nothing," Smith said. "I just need to sit and think for a while. Can you leave me with Butterfly Carcass?"

Brooks sighed. "Butterfly Carcass is giving me a headache. Can you at least turn it down?"

"Yeah, sure," Smith said.

Soon, he'd be able to listen to his music as loudly as he wanted. That was a dark thought. It became even darker when Brooks closed the door and Smith turned off the lights, leaving himself to brood and continue researching time travel. Smith's head was hurting too, mostly from trying to understand general relativity, but also partly from Butterfly Carcass.

Annihilation vacation, a murder on the beach
Annihilation vacation, your death is within reach

Brooks could still hear the amateurish lyrics as he wandered into the kitchen to top off his gin. There, he reached up over the refrigerator (a place his partner would never check or clean) and grabbed an envelope he'd been holding onto for years. He opened it up and slid the note into his hands.

Annihilation vacation, the hotel of your doom
Annihilation vacation, destruction in your room
BODIES IN THE POOOOOOL
NOTHING HERE IS COOOOOL

It was hard to focus on most things with Butterfly Carcass's ambient wailing in the background, but this note was the easiest thing in the world for Brooks to focus on. Every time he had doubts about their relationship, he brought the letter out and read it again. He wondered if he should share it with Smith, if it would help. Then again, it was a Code Fourteen, and any help it could render was surely outweighed by the risks involved in sharing it. A tear ran down his face as he thought about what he knew but couldn't explain.

That memory was the only one of Smith that Brooks had left. He focused, trying to remember the name of that horrible metal band. He knew it was something with a cute animal. Kitten Orgy? No, that wasn't right. Baby Seal Club? That wasn't it either. Smith's face was hazy, and there was some note that made him feel something, but he couldn't remember what it said or to whom it was addressed. He couldn't even remember if it was a good feeling or a bad one. There was just a vague notion that some important letter left him feeling... something.

"Agent Brooks," Stan said.

Brooks blinked as his head swayed gently to and fro. "Y... yes?"

"My name is Stan Sanford. I'm from the year 2202. I need to speak with you."

"The current year is 2014," Brooks said. "A traveler from 2202 is a Code Fourteen. I need to alert my immediate supervisor..."

"I *am* your immediate supervisor," Marsh said.

Brooks continued to sway. "There's a Code Fourteen situation happening. Should I investigate further?"

"What happened to him?" Tangelo asked.

"Memory wipe," Marsh said. "In any case, you said you needed to speak with Agent Smith, so let's go ahead and get out of here and forget we ever came to the—"

"Agent Smith?" Brooks asked.

"Yes, do you know him?" Stan asked, egging him on.

"Smith is the most common last name in the Reticent organization. There are twelve Agent Smiths." He began naming them. "Smith, Anna. Smith, Brendan. Smith, Daryl. Smith, Edward." He paused, almost recognizing something, then continued. "Smith, Gary. Smith, Harriet. Smith, Joanna. Smith, Lyle. Smith, Moira..."

"Okay, we get it," Tangelo said. He turned to Stan and whispered into the President's ear. "This guy is fried. Let's just find the one we came here for."

"No," Stan responded. "I have a feeling Agent Brooks will come in handy dealing with his partner." He added, "And if not, it couldn't hurt to have a cyborg on our side."

"What makes you think he'll be on our side?" Tangelo asked.

"Past experience." Stan smiled.

Marsh butted in. "I really, really have to insist—"

"Have you noticed the giant rift over Manhattan?" Stan asked.

"Of course I have. I'm not—" He intended to finish that sentence with "an idiot," but he actually did feel like an idiot.

"Well it's spreading across time and space, and I need to speak with your agents in order to get answers. This one will do whatever you say, right?"

Marsh nodded.

Stan elaborated. "Well, we need him to help us make Agent Smith cooperate."

Marsh debated with himself. It was the world versus his own neck, and he was fond of his neck. But he knew what he had to do, and steeled his resolve.

"Follow us upstairs, Agent Brooks," he directed.

32 / BANDS THAT DON'T EXIST YET

If there were such a thing as hipster bait, it would look like an antique jukebox. Lemon thus found herself at the end of a long line of skinny jean-clad music connoisseurs, tapping her foot and metaphorically dying for her chance to select Pop Tart & the Activation Energy's "Life of an Olympic Curling Champion." When it came down to just one person ahead of her in line, she became impatient. The perpetrator had a dyed ginger undercut (of course he did) and ironically wore an argyle sweater vest (of course he did). He just couldn't choose between the proven excellence of the Decemberists and a new band out of Topeka called Cone Bone. Because he had no job (of course he didn't), he could only afford to play one.

Lemon muttered under her breath. "Hurry up."

"What do you think?" he asked.

Lemon answered definitively. "The Decemberists are played out. Pick the other one."

He did, and they went their separate ways, him to the bar and her to the elusive jukebox. It was practically for naught; Pop Tart & the Activation Energy didn't exist yet. She sighed, picked another Cone Bone song, took a seat, and sipped at her water. In the few hours she'd been in the past, she'd gained one hundred thirty Twitter followers, forty-one Instagram followers, and received a few dozen messages on both Tinder and the up-and-coming app Tangl. She eyed her prepaid phone and noticed a new Twitter follower: @DukeOfParkSlope.

A quick vetting revealed the account's owner as the indecisive jukebox hog. His profile picture showed him in front of a dumpster, gazing disinterestedly into the distance, and Lemon was smitten.

It seemed the same was true for Duke (No Last Name Given). He liked all thirty of Lemon's tweets and commented on one of her selfies with a heart-eyed emoji. In past decades, Duke might have approached her and struck up a conversation. Because it was the 2010s, he didn't even make eye contact. He remained focused on his phone, awaiting the message that would make personal contact acceptable.

An hour and three hundred potential mates later, Lemon swiped Duke's picture to the right on Tinder.

An hour after that, he sent her a casual message:

Nice song.

33 / TIME TO FLY

Edward Smith (2014 edition) was the slightest bit lucid. He knew that he was being held in Reticent headquarters, and he knew that every time he lashed out someone came and injected him with something that put him to sleep. It was preferable to being awake, really. Smith knew that his partner was dead. He didn't know what the other agents had done to Brooks's body or what they were going to do to his. Most importantly, he knew at this moment that he was unable to move. It wasn't the restraints; those were surprisingly loose. It was paralysis, caused by whatever they'd last injected into him.

One thing he definitely didn't know was the difference between pilgrims and Puritans, and trying to figure it out was where he was determined to focus his mind. To Smith, there was nothing worse than occupying himself with his own thoughts. That was because they trended dark, and not merely 'my partner is dead' dark. Somewhere between remembering his sixth set of parents and trying to repress memories of his sixth set of parents, Smith realized that he probably should have listened to Brooks one of the several dozen times he told Smith he needed therapy. He reined in his focus.

Pilgrims are the Thanksgiving ones, he thought. *Then after they killed the natives they started burning witches. Right? So... what's the difference? You should probably kill yourself. That's dark. No, it's not. It's okay because you can't die. So Puritans have 'pure' in the name, that's probably a clue...*

As it turned out, Smith would have another chance to be berated about his need for therapy. The door opened and, after a minute-long struggle with blindness, Smith's vision cleared and the man who had once personally witnessed the spawning of an orc saw the most improbable thing he'd ever seen: Arturo Brooks was alive and standing next to him. An odd trick of the light combined with the leftover white spots in Smith's eyes to create a halo of sorts above his resurrected partner. Due to the religious undertones, Smith knew he wasn't dreaming. Tangelo freed him from his restraints, while Stan jabbed his leg with a syringeful of something labeled 'Paralysis B Gone.'

Smith jumped up to hug Brooks.

"Agent Edward Smith? Employee ID 7717812?" Brooks asked, pulling away. He recognized the face from his records, but nowhere else. "Have we met?"

The question was a sincere one, but Smith didn't realize it.

"Cut the shit," he said. "How the hell did you survive?"

"Listen," Stan cut in.

"Hudson?" Smith eyed him from top to bottom, noting the significant increase in mass. "How long have I been trapped here?" He looked at Tangelo and Marsh. "Who the hell—"

"I'm your new supervisor," Marsh said.

Brooks tilted his head and repeated himself. "Do I know you?"

Smith's relief turned quickly to pain, which turned quickly to fury. He lunged at Marsh, spitting into the man's face as he shouted. "What did you do to him?"

Marsh was not afforded the opportunity to respond. Before he could open his mouth, Smith's hands gripped his throat. He had never killed a human being before, but—adrenaline racing—he was ready to do so now. He tightened his grip and felt Marsh's blood pulsing as he shoved him against the wall.

A familiar hand grabbed him by the shoulder and pulled him away from his superior. Brooks looked and felt the same, but something about the way he touched his former partner was connectionless and wrong. Smith shook the stranger off and stared into his eyes.

Marsh slid down the wall and settled onto the floor, catching his breath.

Smith's pulse was 101. His blood pressure was 140/93. His estimated age was 38. That's all Brooks saw when he looked at him, and he responded as he was directed to. "Your pulse and blood pressure are high. I suggest you sit down and relax."

"Relax? Are you serious?" Smith turned to Stan, whom he correctly believed to be Hudson, and shouted at him. "You let Brooks take your time machine so he could get himself killed. Then that piece of shit made me immortal. Now I find out he's not dead but he's been turned into a robot—"

"Cyborg," Marsh corrected. "The body is fully his. It's just been enhanced."

Smith didn't understand the difference between robots and cyborgs, and he didn't have the time or energy to think about it. "—A *cyborg* with no memory of who I am or what we had. So what are you here to fuck up this time?"

"I'm not your Hudson Marrow," Stan said. He motioned at his aide. "Tangelo and I are from the year 2202. We're here to find out what you and your partner know about the rift that's consuming everything. It originated here. Right now. In this building."

"Tangelo?" Smith scoffed.

"Yeah, we've already done that," Tangelo said.

"You wanna know what I know about the rift?" Smith asked. "I know I hope it consumes the whole goddamn universe. That's what I know."

"You don't mean that," Stan said.

"I don't?" Smith leaned in. "If you're from 2202, why don't you tell me all about the thrills that await me there? You want me to help. Why should I? Give me a horoscope for the ages." He glanced at Brooks, who awaited orders and remained completely disengaged from the conversation.

Smith's sarcastic demand turned into genuine pleading. "Please. Tell me what I have to look forward to."

Tangelo tried. "Well, future you lives in a mansion..."

"Yeah? With who?"

"Whom," Stan softly corrected. Smith bit his lip and clenched his fist.

Tangelo shrugged. "By yourself..."

"Awesome." Smith kicked over a small trashcan, and several vials of Paralysis B Gone scattered across the floor.

While everyone else was distracted, Travis Marsh reached for the emergency phone above his head. It didn't require him to dial. By coming off its hook, an emergency was activated. TWINKLE TING TWINKLE TWINKLE TING.

"Please," Stan said. "Help us."

"Why?" Smith repeated.

Of all the things Stan could have said, the truth was one of the least persuasive, but he went with it anyway. Smith might appreciate honesty, he figured.

"You're screwed," he said.

TWINKLE TING TWINKLE TWINKLE TING.

"That's what I thought." Smith planted himself back onto his cot and leaned back, hands beneath his head, waiting to be apprehended.

"Let me finish," said Stan.

Smith rolled his eyes.

"You—the 2014 version of you—are screwed. You're going to be stuck here for decades while they experiment on you and torture you. But eventually you'll get out, and your 2090 self will return here. That version of you is going to meet back up with Brooks, and—"

"And what?"

Stan sighed. "I'm going to do everything I can to make sure Brooks remembers who he is and they end up together."

"Well, you let me know how that works out," Smith said. "They're coming for you."

"The *other* you," Stan said, "he won't cooperate. But if we bring his partner to him, he will. Help us get out of this building with him."

"You just said I'm going to be trapped here and tortured for decades," Smith said.

"You will be," Stan acknowledged. "But if you ever want to be with him again, you'll have to take that hit and trust that it will work out eventually."

Smith's eyes shifted back and forth as he processed the information. He decided once again that time travel annoyed him, and that he didn't trust Hudson Marrow. But if there was even the slightest chance that his future self might have a happy ending, he had to go for it. "*Fiiine.*"

He hopped off the cot and led Stan and Tangelo out the door into the hallway. Brooks remained at Marsh's side, watching over his boss. His face was slightly puzzled from the previous exchange. After a moment, the group reached an emergency exit.

"Come on," Smith said to his partner.

"I haven't been authorized to leave," Brooks said.

Smith pulled Brooks's gun from his side and pointed it at Marsh. "Authorize him."

Marsh threw up his hands. "Yes. Agent Brooks. Go. Follow him. Do whatever you want to do." He complained to himself, "I'm *so* screwed."

With that, Brooks followed. So did Marsh. He was as good as dead, but he was going to give the Caribbean a shot, sweat be damned.

At one end of the hallway was the emergency exit. At the other end, a group of armed Reticent guards quickly approached. Smith faced the guards while the others headed through the door.

"When you get to the top, make two lefts," he said.

He knew he was going to be stuck in this building for a long time, so he figured he might as well make it fun. He casually approached the armed agents, borrowed weapon at his side. They were not intimidated.

"Any of you know where I can find a good—"

He fired mid-sentence, managing to kneecap two of the six guards before they returned fire.

Smith fell to the ground, full of holes. He got back up—bullets clinking to the ground as they fell from his abdomen. The guards fired again, sending him back down. It was a cycle that repeated three times before the guards were within arm's reach. He punched one in the dick before two of them restrained him. The dick punchee and the other remaining guard hurried down the corridor.

For a moment, Brooks stared through the emergency exit window at the scene and felt something—not a physical sensation but something inside that didn't make any sense. He ignored it and pressed onward, escorting the time travelers and his talentless boss out of the building.

Outside, the group hurried to where they'd left the time machine, only to find it empty.

"Where's Lemon?" Tangelo asked.

"Who? Marsh asked.

Tangelo looked around the park and repeatedly called for his sister, each shout louder than the previous. He wouldn't find her this way. In her strangeness, she could have run off to experience the subway, a street urinator, McDonalds... There was no way of knowing.

Marsh gestured toward the crowd of Reticent agents gathered outside the building and shushed him.

"You're going to draw attention," he warned.

"Why are you still here?" Stan asked.

Marsh didn't have a good answer. He knew that if he stayed in Reticent headquarters he was doomed to be Nicholas Caged or worse, so he simply followed. It was what he was equipped to do. It hadn't occurred to him that these weren't his friends and he had nothing to do with their mission.

"Do you need any help?" he asked.

Tangelo turned to him. "If you want to help, help me find my sister."

"Sure thing." Marsh loved direction. "Where is she?"

Tangelo put a palm to his forehead. "If I knew where she was, I wouldn't need help finding her." He continued calling her name, to no avail. "Where would a hipster go in 2014?"

Marsh perked up and scurried away.

"Where are you going?" Stan asked.

"I have an idea!" That was a rare event for Marsh, and in his excitement he didn't stop to consider any logistics or consequences. He simply went on his way.

"Come on," Stan said. A group of Reticent guards was headed their way. "We need to get out of here."

"Not without my sister," Tangelo said.

"It's a city of *nine million people* and we have no idea where she is. For now, let's take Agent Brooks to his partner and see what we can get out of him."

Tangelo was uncomfortable with the notion, but Stan was right. Unless Lemon wanted to be found, there was nothing they could do. He gazed into the distance, hoping she was somewhere safe.

34 / MADNESS TAKES ITS TOLL

Against everyone's wishes, Smith had helped himself to Hudson's bar, which was actually just one cupboard under his kitchen sink that contained three bottles of schnapps. This wasn't how a grown man was supposed to drink, but Smith had taken the bottle of Dapper Apple and went with it. The bottle was now empty.

"I came back here to look for Brooksy," he said. "Not to hang around your apartment."

Smith stood in the entrance of the time machine, swinging the empty bottle of schnapps and threatening to take himself back to the future. Hudson, fresh from his confrontation with Veronica, was hardly interested in another argument. Patience was disinterested in conflict altogether. The two anti-conflict members of the team watched the drunken agent dangle from the time machine, swaying back and forth by one arm.

"You know what?" Hudson said. "I came here to put away all the artifacts I've taken, to make sure they didn't accidentally make other people immortal. Now I find out my wife sold nearly everything *and* she let the damn feather shield go for a hundred dollars. Do you know what that was worth?"

"That's a considerable amount of money," Patience noted, imagining the kind of home someone could build with a hundred Spanish dollars.

"That's a cab fare to Manhattan is what that is," Hudson said. "Priceless, immortality-granting artifacts given away for a cab fare to Manhattan. So I'm disinclined to listen to your whining."

"This is whining to you?" Smith asked. "I'm not whining. I'm *pissed*. I could have just stayed home..."

"At *my* home," Hudson corrected.

"Piss off. It's future you's home, and I earned it by putting up with future your shit. I could have stayed there and waited for the universe to end, but you dragged me here. You made a promise. Now keep it."

As if on cue, the second time machine appeared in Hudson Marrow's bedroom. One time machine pushed the boundaries of its square footage; two made the room downright cramped. The second machine landed at an angle, leaning into Hudson's headboard. Out of it stumbled Stan, Tangelo, and the most remarkable thing Smith had ever seen.

Brooks was alive, and he was there. Unconcerned with making a public display, Smith hopped out of the first time machine and rushed his former partner.

"Holy shit. Brooksy..." He looked and felt exactly like Smith remembered him.

He put a hand to his partner's face, and Brooks balked, taking a step back to assess the amount of danger he was in.

"You're alive," Smith gasped.

"You're Agent Smith," Brooks stated. The vitals were a near match (this one's blood pressure was higher) and his display correlated this man with the one he'd seen an hour ago. He proceeded to interrogate Smith. "How did you escape the building? How did you gain weight so quickly?"

"We have a problem," Tangelo said. Behind him, Hudson's headboard cracked under the weight of the time machine.

"You're damn right we have a problem," Smith said. "What's wrong with him?"

"There's nothing wrong with any of my systems," Brooks said.

Smith choked over his words. "Your *systems*?"

"The Reticent did some work on him," Stan said. "He's been upgraded with cybernetic—"

Smith took a step backward. "You brought me back here

so I could experience *this*? You—"

A moment that had been building for decades finally came, and Smith snapped. "To prove to me... that life is worth living... you brought me back to the year Brooks died so I could find out he's actually alive and has no memory of me." He laughed, then grabbed the nearest piece of pretentious artwork—a stone shaped like either a person or a tree—and threw it across the room. He paced along the bed, still chuckling. "It never stops, does it? If you're not beaten half to death by your parents, you're fucked over by some shitty fosters. If you're not watching the love of your life bleed out in front of you, he turns into a robot and forgets who you are. If you're not spending thirty years being tortured, you're spending fifty years thinking about being tortured. And guess what! You're immortal now so no matter what you do, the shit train just keeps on rolling! Choo choo!" Smith dropped to the floor, simultaneously laughing and crying. The headboard finally gave way and the time machine fell to its side, which made Smith laugh and cry harder.

Whatever slight feeling Brooks had felt back at Reticent headquarters returned. It wasn't an actionable feeling, but it left him staring at his former partner, trying to interpret the man's contradictory emotions.

"We have a problem," Tangelo repeated, looking at Hudson and ignoring the hunkered heap of human despair. "Lemon is missing."

Stan agreed. "We need to find her."

"What about the rift?" Hudson asked.

"We need to do this first," Stan said.

Hudson nodded, trusting himself.

At the moment Hudson nodded, an epiphany struck Stan.

"I know where she is," he said.

"What?" Tangelo asked.

"I remember finding her when I was you," he said, pointing at Hudson.

Smith briefly removed his head from his hands. "What the fuck?" He was so very tired of time travel.

"Do you not remember stopping the rift?" Tangelo asked.

"No, I guess I wasn't around for that," said Stan.

Smith leaned his head back into the wall and began cackling. "Of course you weren't."

"Are you all right, sir?" Patience asked.

Smith cackled harder.

"Your sister is in Brooklyn," Stan said, ignoring the crazy elephant in the room.

"Of course," Tangelo said. "Who wants to come with me?"

"I'll go," Stan said, pushing at the side of his time machine, trying to right it.

"Hey, I have a bright idea," Smith said. "Instead of being a time traveling freak show, why don't you take a cab?"

Hudson considered that. "You know, he has a point. It's a lot less conspicuous if you're trying not to let everyone in on the fact that we created a time machine."

"Fine," Stan said. "I want the cyborg for backup, though."

Brooks remembered what Marsh had said. *Do whatever you want to do.*

"I'll accompany you," he said. Solving a missing persons report was 100% what he wanted to do, thanks to some clever programming.

Stan spoke to Hudson. "Watch over Agent Smith and make sure he doesn't do anything stupid."

"Like hell," Smith interjected. Under no circumstance was he going to continue to be babysat by pompous man-child Hudson Marrow. Under no circumstance was he going to be sidelined with the delicate pilgrim. Under no circumstance was he going to sit around and let these people save a world that didn't deserve to be saved. He stood up and grouped himself with the search party.

"I really think you should stay here," Stan said, not wanting the maniacal agent's company.

Smith glowered at him. "I really think you should fuck off back to the twenty-third century, but what do I know?"

"I agree with Stan," Brooks said. "Your pulse and blood pressure are dangerously high."

"There's no such thing as 'danger' to me. You get that, right?" Smith said. "They didn't take away your ability to process facts, did they? I'm immortal."

"You know, we don't know whether that effect is permanent," Stan said. "You were able to age yourself a bit, however small—"

"All the more reason to put myself in danger," Smith answered. "It's been seventy-some years, though, so I think my odds are pretty good... er, bad."

There was—again—no arguing with Smith when he was like this and Smith was—again—always like this. The group acquiesced and, after a brief ninety-minute wait for a cab, they were on their way to Brooklyn.

35 / ONE HELL OF A FARE

For seventy more minutes the four of them sat, crammed into a yellow cab, Smith up front with the poor driver, while Stan, Tangelo, and Brooks took the backseat.

"It sure is nice to be leaving *Staten Island*, isn't it?" Smith asked, trying to provoke a response from his partner.

He glanced over his shoulder to confirm that there was no response. "Given your history, I'm sure you couldn't wait to get out of there. Right, Brooksy?"

"Why do you keep adding a 'y' to the end of my name?"

"Fuck me," said Smith, exasperated.

"That would be against code 1.14.9," Brooks said.

Smith again took to cackling maniacally. "Jesus Christ," he muttered between laughs.

Tangelo turned to Stan. "Where exactly are we going?"

"Somewhere around where Crown Heights meets Bed-Stuy," Stan said. "I think we found her in a bar or something. I may be immortal, but my memory's not great."

"Hey, looks like we're gonna be near our house," Smith said. "That ring any bells for you?"

Brooks shook his head. "My home is Reticent headquarters."

Smith turned around and stared at his partner through a gap in the plexiglass that divided the cab.

"No. It's not," he said.

Smith didn't know why he was attempting to reach Brooks when it was obviously hopeless, but he kept doing it. "You lived with me at 55 Decatur Street. You hated the fact that there was no dishwasher. I thought about getting one for Christmas once, but then I realized that's a really shitty gift. It's like saying 'do some chores for me' and—" He caught himself rambling. "That's really not the point."

Brooks tilted his head, confused as to what the point was supposed to be.

"The point is we lived together," Smith said. "Not as roommates, either. You don't remember any of that?"

"No." The words 'Butterfly Carcass' came to the forefront of Brooks's mind, but because the words didn't make any sense he ignored them.

"Try?" Smith pleaded.

"I don't understand what you want me to do," Brooks said.

"55 Decatur Street," Smith said, turning to the driver.

"We're looking for a bar," Tangelo corrected.

"Five minute detour," Smith said.

"My sister is missing!"

Smith rolled his eyes. "Your sister's fine! She's in Brooklyn, not the fucking Gaza Strip. Also, she's immortal. Let me take a detour for five fucking minutes so I can try to—"

"You have all the time in the world for that," Tangelo said.

"No, I *have had* all the time in the world."

The annoyed diver chimed in. "Decatur Street or not?"

"Yes," Stan said, sighing.

Tangelo objected. "But—"

"I think we need to let him have the detour," Stan said. "And by 'I think' I mean 'I know.' We're going to find your sister. Relax."

They arrived minutes later at a building that was roped off with DO NOT CROSS tape. A fire had consumed half the block, but it ended right at the Brooks/Smith home so their building was only half-charred. Smith chuckled when he saw that it was practically divided in two. On the right side, the windows were blown out and haloed with black. On the left, everything appeared to be fine.

"I don't think we should go in there," Tangelo said, stepping out of the cab.

"I don't think so either," Smith said. "You and John Titor here can stay put. Brooksy and I will go inside."

"Who is—" Tangelo started, but didn't care to finish.

"Is it wise for us to go inside?" Brooks asked. "The building looks like a hazard."

"Newsflash: I'm immortal and you're a robot. Nothing is a hazard," Smith said.

"That's not true. There are sixty-three ways to destroy a cybernetic—"

"Come on," Smith said, grabbing his partner by the hand and dragging him up the stairs.

If he couldn't get Brooks back, Smith didn't know what he was going to do. His go-to solution was suicide, but since over a hundred attempts in fifty years hadn't worked, it seemed unlikely to work now. He considered therapy once more, but shrugged the idea off.

The door was jammed. It seemed the fire had melted something in the knob and it wouldn't come open. Smith fussed with it for a good minute before asking Brooks to take care of it. The newly minted cyborg pulled the entire door off its frame with ease, and while Smith should have been thinking about how frightening that was, what he really thought about was how turned on the act made him. He was a sick man.

Inside, the living room was a disaster. Smith immediately took to the Nornäs bookcase, looking for something that could be salvaged. He brushed some soot off the game of LIFE and presented it to his partner.

"Remember this?" he asked.

Brooks shook his head. "No."

For some time, Smith scurried from one place to another, presenting memento after memento in hopes he could unlock just one memory. A picture from the Reticent holiday party garnered no reaction. A copy of *To Kill a Mockingbird* had the same lack of effect. Smith's Ralex watch inspired nothing, not even a look of mild contempt.

"What are we looking for?" Brooks asked, confused. "I

don't understand how this relates to stopping the dimensional rift."

"Dimensional?" Smith asked. "Who said anything about dimensions?"

"That's what it is, so why are we here?"

Smith laughed and broke down into tears again. In decades of life, he had cried maybe twenty times by his own estimate. In the last day, it had happened on a dozen separate occasions. He was astutely aware of just how fragile his mind had become, and how little the bourbon had dulled the pain.

"Yeah, this was stupid," he said.

"If you tell me what we're looking for, I may be able to help," Brooks said.

"You don't remember this place at all?" Smith asked.

Brooks had picked out everything that surrounded them, from the curtains to the couch to the picture frames to the type of hand soap sitting at the kitchen sink. He had picked it all because Smith didn't care. In his mind, soap was soap and picture frames were picture frames. But every time Brooks picked something out, he had done so with care. Different woods were symbolic of different things, apparently. Different soap scents could affect the mood, apparently. Cotton Blossom was supposed to elicit cheer. It was failing.

Brooks glanced around the room and felt nothing.

"I think I've been here before," he said, "but I'm not sure when or why."

"This was our home," Smith said, seating himself on the charred sofa.

"I don't remember," Brooks said. "Maybe this place didn't mean as much to me as you think it did."

"Don't say that," Smith insisted, sure that it did mean as much to Brooks. Probably more. "Just look around." He leaned back and gave the burnt furniture a contemptuous sniff. "Look at everything. Please."

Brooks obliged. Moving into the less burnt area of the

house, he checked the kitchen counters, inside the cabinets, inside the fridge. That last one was a mistake. Without power, everything inside it had spoiled and it unleashed the odor of rotting fish and sour milk. He slammed the door shut. With that, a letter fell from the top of the fridge: a piece of 92 bright copy paper that bore the wrinkles of something that had been folded and unfolded hundreds of times. There was some ash on it, but it was otherwise unharmed by the blaze. Brooks plucked it from the floor and began reading.

36 / TIME AFTER TIME

Global warming hadn't hit hard yet in 2004, but it was still damn warm. Despite the fact that it was August and eighty degrees out, even in the middle of the night, Arturo Brooks shivered. Watching one's entire family be ripped apart by undead monsters could do that to a person.

Agent Burroughs had just finished explaining debriefing procedures when she wrapped a blanket around the traumatized young man and began escorting him toward the Reticent's mobile headquarters near the stage.

"Is he still freaking out?" Smith asked, pretending he was calm and not also totally freaked out by the fact that he'd just seen his future self.

"Obviously," Burroughs said. "How can you be so insensitive?"

"It comes naturally," Smith said.

She spoke softly to Brooks, pointing at the mobile unit. "There. Can you make it over there? I need to discuss something with my partner."

Brooks nodded. He wasn't sure he could make it two hundred yards without any support, but he forced himself onward. While Burroughs berated Smith in the background, Brooks walked. Short step by short step, he walked, eyes straight ahead, just like he'd been instructed. He reminded himself to avoid looking down at the gore. Then, as these things go, he looked down.

Amongst blood-spattered sidewalks and dirty corpses, something bright white stood out. It was pristine, untouched by human or wraith fluids—as if it had been placed there just for him. Brooks knelt down, grabbed the piece of 92 bright copy paper, and shakily stood himself back up. He read the note as he walked even more slowly than before.

Dear Self,

That sucked, didn't it? I know what you're thinking. One: you want to fuck Burroughs. I'd tell you not to do it, but I know you will. Whatever. Go for it.

The other thing you're thinking is: did I really just see that? Yes, you did. I'm going to label this with years so you understand. You (2004) saw yourself (2014) crying over the dead body of 2014 Brooks, the guy you just met in 2004. It's some "City on the Edge of Forever" shit. So fuck that guy, right? He's going to die. No point getting to know him.

<u>Wrong</u>. Arturo Brooks is the best thing that will ever happen to you. You know how shitty life has been so far? Of course you do. Well, it's only going to get shittier, so buckle the fuck up. But before it does, you're going to spend the best ten years of your life with that man. You're going to care so much about him it disgusts you, and it's going to be worth it. Because when things get shitty (seriously, they are going to get so shitty) he's the only good thing you'll have to look back on.

I know I'm not the most trustworthy person in the world, but trust me. Yes, he's going to die, but love Arturo Brooks so much it makes you want to puke, then love him more than that. Then actually puke, I guess. He's the one who's going to end up bleeding out in a field. Show him a great time before that.

Oh, and don't fucking tell him about this. Seriously. You know how he gets. Well, you don't yet, but I do. Don't give him anything else to worry about. He has enough problems.

Be you soon,
E. S.

Brooks didn't know what to think or what to do. Four hours earlier, he had been a senior in the chemistry program at CUNY. He had a father, he had a sister, and he had no idea there were creatures of the night waiting to destroy people like him. He had no idea the Reticent did anything more than medical research. He had no idea there was such a thing as time travel. Now he knew all of those things, as well as the fact that he was going to die in Willowbrook Park ten years in the future. Inside Arturo Brooks, a mental countdown of his lifespan began. There were so many things he needed to do—find meaningful work, start a family—and there was so little time.

Epiphanies don't come around very often; if they did, they'd be altschmerzanies.* Brooks stood still for several minutes, staring at the letter. He read it once, then twice, then a third time. With each successive study of the words, a voice in his head called out louder. *Butterfly Carcass*, it said. The voice still didn't make any sense. Brooks let his hands fall as he looked into the living room. Smith lay on the sofa, head in hands, making a sound that was halfway between chuckling and sobbing. The urge to go to him came over Brooks. Instead of heeding it, he stood and pondered the meaning behind it. Clearly there was something to what the irritable agent had been saying, but did it matter? He wasn't the Smith that Brooks had known. He was from the future. Even if they'd once had something in common, they didn't now.

A loud CRASH filled the room.

"Door was open, asshole," said Smith, who assumed the source was Stan or Tangelo.

---

* One for the linguists.

While Brooks continued scouring his mind for fragments of memories, Smith became suddenly and mildly endangered. John Wilmington of Salem execution fame broke through the only unbroken window in the living room. Within seconds, his hands were wrapped around Smith's neck. He obviously hadn't received the memo about Smith's immortality.

Brooks had, essentially, received that memo. But even knowing his former partner would be fine, he was galvanized into action against the attacker. He stuffed the letter into his pocket, rushed into the living room, and shot the man in the head.

Smith gasped for air as the attacker fell to the floor. Death may have been impossible, but being strangled still hurt like hell. He choked out a short "thanks."

The bullet didn't end John Wilmington's life. After only a few seconds, his body pushed the bullet out of his skull and healed the tissue it had damaged. Brooks, remembering something he'd been trained in, walked away from the scene and headed toward the basement.

"Oh, don't worry about it," Smith said. "I'll fend him off with my bare hands."

He attempted to do just that, and soon found himself being strangled again. He reflected that he needed to improve his hand-to-hand combat skills; in the last seventy years they'd gotten more than a little rusty. As his airflow stopped, Smith became dizzy. His throat tightened and his chest throbbed like it could burst from the pressure.

The swift swing of an axe rescued him from a temporary death, and Brooks stood over his partner, smiling ever so slightly.

"You know he'll come back," Smith said between coughs.

"Only if his head is put back onto his neck," Brooks answered. He picked up the head in question and walked it over to the kitchen, placing it in the sink. It couldn't make its way back to Wilmington's body from there, and the agents could take a breather.

"Are you okay?" Brooks asked.

"No worse than usual," Smith said. He noticed that the other man was staring at him. "What did I do?"

"Nothing. There's something I'm trying to remember."

Smith jolted up. This was exactly what he wanted: just a sliver of hope that Brooks could return to him. He grabbed the man's arm and pulled him close, tilting his head just so in order to bring Brooks in for a kiss. It was soft and brief, and it confused the cyborg.

"I don't think that's it," Brooks said, taking a seat on the blackened sofa.

Smith was let down by life... again. Then life surprised him.

"I loved you," Brooks said. He pulled the crinkled letter from his pocket and unfolded it, leaning in so that his partner could read it. "I don't remember why, but I know that I loved you."

"Yeah, I don't know why either," Smith said. As he scanned the letter, his jaw very nearly hit the floor. "I wrote this for myself." Of course, he thought, his past self had never received it. Time never changed. He figured that it had been lost in the chaos following the wraith attack. Instead, it had always been with his partner. "You had this for ten years?"

"I think so," Brooks said. Being only a few days old, he had a very poor concept of time.

"You knew you were gonna die a horrible death and you stayed with the only person you knew would be there for that. Why wouldn't you try to change the future?"

"I don't know. I don't remember."

"Try harder," Smith demanded.

"Time is a closed loop. What has happened will happen. It wouldn't have made sense," Brooks said.

"You didn't know that in 2004. Try harder," Smith said,

louder than before.

Suddenly, Brooks's mind was in Willowbrook Park. His father and sister were dead and chunks of their entrails littered the sidewalk. Warm blood ran down the side of his face. In the distance, someone screamed.

"Fuck fuck fuck," he said. If this was what he was missing, he didn't want his memories back.

"*Not that one.* Don't think about that one," Smith said. He began rattling off more pleasant memories. "Uh, Philly, 2011. Aruba, 2009." Noticing his partner's glazed-over eyes, he became flustered and just repeated himself. "Aruba, 2009?"

"I didn't care if I died," Brooks said. He appeared to be in a trance as his mind recalled what it was supposed to have forgotten. "I'd lost my entire family. I'd lost my entire life. Knowing you'd be there for my death only made me want to be near you more. I kind of... wanted you to get me killed?"

Smith, the death-wishingest person in the world, teared up hearing about Brooks's death wish. "And after that?"

"I loved you," Brooks repeated.

The cyborg stared at the half-burnt Nornäs. On it, the game of LIFE still stood proudly. That was it. It was now the item he needed to remember it all. One drunken night of IKEA furniture building had become a symbol of Brooks's second chance at life. He looked at it and memories came back to him faster than he could process them. Philly, 2011. Aruba, 2009. The holiday party. Ralex watches and *To Kill a Mockingbird.* The alley blowjob.* The words Butterfly Carcass finally made sense. Every time Smith had needlessly used the word 'fuck.' It was all there. He practically dove onto his partner, locking onto lips that were familiar but new.

"I love you," Brooks said.

Smith couldn't handle that. After a century of torture—

---

* They weren't all classy memories.

first living in dread of his partner's death then living for decades without him—he had a happy ending. The world was not just. The world was never just.

Something's gonna go wrong, he thought.

Something always went wrong. Like, giant dimensional tear wrong. He finally had his happiness and the world was going to be consumed by a creeping void. Instead of responding to his partner, Smith bawled as every awful moment flooded his mind. "I—"

"I know," Brooks said. "I mean, I don't know exactly what you've been through, but... it's over now. I'm here and you're here and we're both going to live forever so—"

"Don't say that. You're gonna jinx it."

"You think we can be jinxed any worse?" Brooks said, chuckling softly through tears of his own.

Smith wasn't sure what to say, so he diverted. "There's a rift... and we should do something about that guy." He pointed at the headless corpse. "Need to figure out why he was here and—"

"Eddie?"

"What?"

"Fuck that guy."

37 / ARE WE THERE YET?

Tangelo and Stan tired of waiting for Brooks and Smith to reconcile or do whatever it was they were doing. Because the thing they were doing could very well have been having loud, kinky human-on-cyborg sex in the middle of the living room, they didn't check. At one point they thought they heard a crash, but for the same reason avoided bringing themselves toward it. Besides, Tangelo needed to find his sister.

"What's the most hipster-y bar around here?" Tangelo asked as they walked the streets.

Stan glanced from bar to bar. "Take your pick."

One was noted for its artisanal gin. Another boasted 263 taps. Why a bar needed that many taps was neither questioned nor explained.

"Is there any place that might hold special meaning for her?" Stan asked.

Tangelo thought hard. The problem was that he never really paid attention when his sister was talking. All she ever wanted to discuss was history, and Tangelo felt that looking back was pointless. The two had little but blood in common, and it was beginning to show. As he replayed conversations they'd had over the years, racking his brain for anything that might have been relevant, the answer appeared before them: a small bar called Pucker Up with a lemon-shaped sign made from repurposed coasters. Stan poked his companion's shoulder to make him take note.

"Well, that's worth a shot," Tangelo said.

Also worth a shot was the nine dollars and eighty-three cents that Travis Marsh had just passed along to the bartender. Tonight, he was going to drink like it was the end of the world, not just because the Reticent were going to destroy him for letting Brooks escape but because they were literally facing the end of the world. He said as much to anyone who would listen, which was just the bartender. She had a vested interest in listening to her customers' insane ramblings. Marsh was the fourth doomsdayer she'd encountered this week, but she didn't let it get her down. Those types tipped well because they knew they couldn't take the money with them when they were hauled off by the antichrist.

"Puritans," he scoffed for the seventeenth time. He knew everything and he still couldn't believe it. The Puritans were never the bad guys. Okay, maybe in *The Scarlet Letter* and *The Crucible*, but never in the twenty-first century.

In the corner of the room, Lemon fed a jukebox some money. Tangelo spotted her and rushed to her side. Stan followed at a much, much slower pace.

"What are you doing?" Tangelo asked.

Lemon looked over her shoulder. "Trying to play some Cone Bone."

"What are you doing in a bar? You're seventeen."

"Fake ID," she said.

Tangelo raised his voice. "You've been in 2014 for six hours and you already have a fake ID?"

Lemon shrugged and glanced at a ginger sitting in the corner. "Duke helped me out."

"Duke?" Tangelo didn't ask. "We're going home," he said, grabbing her arm.

"Let me go," she complained as he led her past the bar toward the exit.

"Puritans," Marsh grumbled.

Overhearing that brought Stan to a halt that would have been screeching if he were an automobile. As he was not (not yet anyway), the halt was soundless aside from his words.

"What did you say?" Stan asked the man at the bar.

Lemon shrugged her brother off, and the two of them joined Stan to find out why he'd stopped.

"Thirty three years," Marsh complained. "Thirty three

years of service and it comes down to..." Through some drunk and blurry lenses, Marsh suddenly realized the man speaking to him was the one who had broken into the building earlier. "You!"

"Hi," Stan said.

"You tricked me," Marsh grumbled. He downed his shot and clinked the glass against the counter.

"Another?" the bartender asked.

Marsh made a rolling motion with his fingers in response and the bartender poured another.

"It doesn't matter," Marsh said. "We're all screwed anyway. At least I'm at Pucker Up instead of work for the end of the world."

"Is this about the rift?" Stan asked.

"It's not a rift," Marsh said. "It's not an accident. They wanted it this way." He finished his shot and made the same finger rolling gesture to receive another.

"Maybe you should slow down," Tangelo said.

"Maybe you should... speed up," Marsh stupidly retorted.

Stan was a proficient interpreter of the drunk language, and he tried to explain what he believed Marsh was getting at. "The Reticent opened it on purpose?"

Marsh nodded. He had finally hit his wall, and sipped only half the shot that was now in front of him. He stared at the other half, squelched a burp, then leaned back and groaned. "Yeah. I didn't know until about an hour ago."

"What happened?" Stan asked.

"Email..."

"You got an email. What did it say?"

"Somebody made a typo... sent something to tmarsh2 instead of tmarsh3... somebody named Thaddeus Marsh... never even heard of him..."

"What did it say?" Stan repeated, insisting the drunken man give him an answer.

"They're staging a coup," he said. "I guess. I don't know...

bunch of Puritans opening a hole to another dimension to suck everyone in." He reluctantly finished his shot. "Obviously it's working... giant hole over Manhattan."

"We need to get back in there," Stan said.

Tangelo shook his head. "They know who we are now. They're not gonna let us walk in after we stole their cyborg."

"Actually," Stan said, "they might."

38 / THE GAME OF LIFE

Brooks and Smith sat in their singed living room, staring at the headless body on the floor. Smith poked at it with a melted flyswatter as Brooks rubbed his partner's back.

"It doesn't make sense, does it?" Smith asked.

"What, sitting here instead of doing something useful?"

Smith gave him a look that said "yes" but continued. "He bled out all over the place. If we put the head on, he'll heal himself, but where does the new blood come from?"

"His decapitated head *reattaches itself* and the blood is the part you're not getting?" Brooks asked.

Smith shrugged. "You know what else I don't get?"

"Why we're still just sitting here?" Brooks laughed.

"No," Smith said. "You."

Brooks frowned. "You don't get me?"

"Specifically the robot thing."

"I'm not a robot," Brooks said.

"You're basically a robot."

"I'm not a robot. I'm me."

Smith tilted his head and pointed out an inconvenient fact. "You ripped the front door off the house."

"Well... who's to say I couldn't do that before?"

"What else did they change?" Smith asked.

Brooks didn't want to talk about it. "I don't know. I guess I'm stronger and I have this HUD now, but I'm me. I'm skin and bones. I don't know..." He cringed. "If you think it's bad for you, trust me it feels a lot worse on this end."

Smith went silent and absorbed that comment. He knew a thing or two about suddenly becoming immortal, and he knew a thing or two about having his bodily autonomy violated, but he didn't know the first thing about realizing your body wasn't your own.

"Can we talk about you?" Brooks asked.

"Why?"

"You're over a hundred years old," Brooks said. "I think that's worth talking about."

"It's not." Smith knew what was coming, and he tried to deflect the embarrassment.

"You've seen and done so much. I want to hear about it."

Smith scoffed.

Brooks insisted. "Eddie?"

"I did *nothing*, okay?" Smith looked away, not wanting to see Brooks's face when he revealed the information. "I was held captive for thirty-some years and I don't remember any of it. Then I paraded through time and space trying to kill myself. That's... how I spent my summer vacation."

Brooks reacted with concern. "You don't remember thirty years?"

"I... I guess I kind of remember." Smith corrected himself. "I don't *want* to remember."

Brooks understood that sentiment all too well. He stood from the couch. "Let's go rescue you then."

Smith also rose, and his hands navigated to his hips in a show of disbelief. "What?"

"Let's go rescue you so you never live through that."

"That's not how this works," Smith said. "You know that's not how this works."

"But who says? What if we do it?"

"We don't succeed. We can't." Smith began fuming. "Do you really need to learn that lesson again after what happened the last time you tried to change history?"

Brooks shook his head. "I know. But, what? You're supposed to suffer for three decades? We just go on living our lives like the version of you that actually belongs in this year isn't being tortured?"

"It's okay," Smith said.

"It's not okay," Brooks said.

Smith took his partner's hand. "No, it is. If I had to be tortured so I could come back here and find you, it was worth it." He curled his lip. "Ugh. Did I just say that?"

"You did." Brooks planted a kiss on his partner's cheek.

"I take it back then," said Smith.

"Seventy years and you haven't changed at all."

Smith thought about a few things. "I wouldn't say that..."

As he prepared to expound on those changes—specifically that he regretted never starting the family Brooks always wanted—the two men were interrupted by the sound of a teenager shouting "Sweet Xenu!"

Lemon stood in the doorway in front of her brother and Stan, staring at the headless corpse and the bloody axe lying next to it.

"You're a scientologist?" Smith wondered.

Lemon scoffed. "No, Lunans just say that ironically."

Stan pushed her aside and confronted the axe murderers. "What the hell did you do?"

Brooks explained. "This guy came in and attacked us."

"Turns out he's one of the immortals," Smith added. "He's not dead, but we left his head in the sink for the time being."

"Oh, well that's okay then," Tangelo said. He directed his next words to his sister. "Don't look at it."

"Too late. Already did," Lemon said. "Still am."

"The Reticent sent someone to retrieve you?" Stan asked.

"I don't think he was after either of us," Brooks said. "Not really. I think he was looking for something. He seemed surprised we were here."

"So clear out the block with a fire and look for—" Stan had nothing. "Look for what?"

Smith shrugged. "I don't think we had anything special."

Brooks responded to that with a pointed side-eye.

"He's not a robot anymore?" Tangelo asked.

"I was never a robot!" Brooks snapped.

"Anyway," Smith said, "you know what I meant. What the

hell would anyone want from here?"

Stan inched toward the kitchen. "You said you left the head in the sink?"

When he made it there, he saw John Wilmington's face staring back at him. Unlike Smith, he recognized the importance of the man. "Hey, you could have mentioned that it was one of the Puritans from your photograph."

"Is he?" Smith asked.

"Do you have zero capacity for facial recognition?" Stan asked.

Smith shrugged.

"I'm confused," Brooks said.

Stan took that opportunity to briefly summarize why he, Tangelo, Lemon, and Smith had traveled from the future in the first place, since it appeared Smith hadn't bothered. Once Brooks knew they were chasing answers about the rift, and that somehow a group of immortal Puritans was connected to it, something in his programming clicked.

"I know this," he said, staring blankly at nothing. "I know the plan. I was supposed to be part of it."

"What is it?" Smith said.

"I'm trying to tell you," Brooks said.

Everyone waited for a moment.

"You're not saying anything," Smith noted.

"I know," Brooks said. He literally couldn't say anything. Something in his mind blocked him from speaking about the plan. It also blocked him from saying that something was blocking him from speaking about the plan.

Luckily, Stan was capable of translating. "Whatever they did to him won't let him talk about it."

"Shit," said Smith.

"I have a plan," Stan said, "but you're not going to like it."

Smith raised his brow. "Let me guess: we waltz right back into HQ and try to stop them?"

"Kind of..."

"Fuck that." Smith prepared a lengthy rant about the Reticent and how he planned to never set foot in their building again, but he was interrupted.

"Travis said it was a coup," Stan said. "So we don't have to take down the whole organization or anything, just find the people responsible."

"Who the hell is Travis?" Smith asked.

"Travis Marsh. Your new boss," Stan said.

"Why the hell do I have a new boss if I'm stuck being tortured?"

Brooks, who had been squinting and straining to recall details, finally grabbed hold of one and changed the subject. "We should talk to Werewith."

"Are you insane?" Smith asked.

"She doesn't know about this," Brooks said. "She's not one of them."

Smith couldn't believe that. "You're telling me there's a legitimately evil scheme going on inside the Reticent and Werewith *isn't* involved?"

Brooks nodded. "The doctor who worked on me was doing something against her direction. I..." He found himself blocked from speaking again. "Damn it."

"Beep once if it has something to do with Talos 4," Smith said.

Stan chuckled.

"What are you talking about?" Brooks asked.

"It's *Star Trek*." Smith's head sank in defeat. "Never mind."

"Who is Agatha Werewith?" Lemon asked.

"Someone you never, ever want to meet."

39 / LET IT BURN

Hudson's apartment smelled heavily of burnt microwave popcorn. After the first overly salted bag, Patience had become fond of the food and requested it for every meal. She was so fond of it that the entire apartment constantly smelled like fake butter. With a little bit of convincing, she allowed Hudson to teach her how to microwave her own. She had the process down, mostly, except for the last time when she accidentally pressed the "Reheat Dinner" button instead of the "Popcorn" button. That had led to the burnt smell (and burnt popcorn, but she had eaten that without complaint). She sat on the couch, continuing her way through *AMERICA: The History*. She had made it up to 1861 and, even though the ending had been spoiled for her, looked forward to seeing how the Civil War would unfold.

When nobody answered the doorbell, Brooks broke through the door dramatically. Patience looked over, saw that it was her rescuers, and turned back to the television. She was adapting to the twenty-first century well.

The men began searching the apartment for its owner.

"I told him I should have taken the time machine to Brooklyn," Stan said. The cab ride had taken eighty minutes. They were eighty minutes closer to the end of the world.

"Where's Hudson?" Smith asked, exiting the bedroom.

"He left, sir," Patience said.

"He left you alone?" Brooks asked, appalled. "What for?"

"I believe he said something about going to see his wife."

"Awesome," Smith said.

"Oh, I remember that," Stan said, cringing. "I... he's begging her to take him back. It's embarrassing."

"We don't need him anyway," Tangelo said.

"We don't need you either," Smith noted.

"We don't need anyone but Patience," Stan said, "but the more hands on deck the better."

Patience looked up from the screen, wide-eyed. "Excuse me?"

"We need to bring you back to the Reticent," Stan said.

Patience sank as far into the sofa as she could. Going back to the place where she was torn apart and put back together over and over again was not her idea of a good time. Maybe, she thought, if she could sink far enough into the couch she would be absorbed and they would be unable to retrieve her. This was not the case.

Brooks approached and attempted to ease her mind. "Just think of it—"

"There's no good way to think of it," Smith interrupted, taking his partner by surprise. Brooks could hardly fathom that Smith was entering an emotional conversation with a teenager, but there it was. Smith sat down next to the girl. "I know what they did to you. They did that and worse to me for thirty years. But I'm still here."

"I don't wish to spend thirty years there," she said.

"You're not going to. Nobody knew they had me," Smith lied. The truth was that the people who could have saved him didn't care to. "Brooksy and I aren't going to let them keep you, okay?"

She nodded.

"Do you trust us?" he asked.

She nodded again.

"Good," Smith said. "We need to get out of here now."

Brooks stood silent and flabbergasted.

The group filed into Hudson's bedroom. To their disappointment, the inventor had taken his creation out for a spin, leaving only the machine that Stan and the Joneses had brought from the future. Piling Stan, Tangelo, Lemon, Patience, Brooks, and Smith into a booth built for four presented a challenge. Brooks wedged himself between the booth's table and Smith's lap and Patience slid in next to them, tucking herself under Brooks's arm. On the other side of the booth, nobody wanted to sit on Stan's lap. Tangelo offered the seat to Lemon and stood on the tabletop, holding onto a convenient subway-style handgrip at the top of the machine. He spread his legs just so they wouldn't touch any of the levers or dials on the table.

"Don't move," Stan said.

"I won't," Tangelo insisted. It wouldn't have been easy in his hunched position, and he wasn't about to cause the machine to send them back to the Dark Ages or vaporize them or any other awful thing it was capable of doing.

The glow and its accompanying sound let everyone know that the machine was departing. Within seconds, it was again parked outside Reticent headquarters.

Smith made a gagging noise, and Brooks tried to free himself. It was no use; he was wedged in and it would take a few seconds to get out. That few seconds was all the time Smith needed to throw up on the back of his partner's coat. On the other side of the booth, Lemon dropped out of the machine and immediately puked on the ground.

"Hey!" Smith said, feeling a sense of camaraderie.

Brooks glared at him.

"It's not just me," Smith boasted before making another gagging noise.

Tangelo, Stan, and Patience filed out of the machine. Brooks finally got unstuck and slid across the booth to make his exit as well. When he escaped, he pulled his coat off and tossed it on the ground.

"You're just gonna leave your coat there?" Tangelo asked.

"Eh, some vagrant will take it," Smith said, exiting the machine. He puked a little more.

"The love of my life, everyone," Brooks proclaimed.

40 / A MEETING WITH AGATHA

Agatha Werewith was not amused, and when she was not amused she took to belittling her employees. One such session was well overdue for Travis Marsh, and he had been dragged back to headquarters from Pucker Up to face up to his offenses.

"I told you," he hiccupped. "I didn't kill Agent... Wilmington."

"Obviously not. He's not dead. Here's how I see it. I sent him to retrieve you and he ended up decapitated in the home of a subordinate you stole from this building."

"I didn't do it... I went to the bar," Marsh complained. "You should... thanking me. Damn Puritans trying... end the world."

Before she could interrogate him further, Marsh passed out. His head landed in his arms and within seconds he was snoring. Werewith considered the various tortures her organization was capable of, but she couldn't decide which one would be best for him.

Do we still do the thing with the snakes? she wondered.

It didn't matter. If they didn't still do the thing with the snakes, she would make them do the thing with the snakes. She had that power.

Werewith's phone rang, and she berated the woman at the information desk for daring to call her with "urgent business." She decided what was urgent business, damn it.

"So help me," she said. "If this turns out to be anything less than the gravest crisis to ever hit this organization, I will murder you myself."

The words on the other end of the line convinced her that it was, in fact, a grave crisis (possibly the gravest), and five minutes later she begrudgingly invited the entire time-traveling crew into her office after tipping Marsh out her third floor window to the street below. He landed with a modest thud.

"The information desk tells me you're here to return the Puritan and the cyborg," she said.

"Yes," Stan agreed.

"And there is, of course, a catch?"

"You need to stop your people from destroying the universe," said Stan.

There it was. All of their drama summarized into one brief sentence. Unfortunately, Werewith's response was nowhere near as loaded with gravitas.

"I have no idea what you're talking about," she said. "Now give me back my property."

"It's illegal to own people," Patience said. "*AMERICA: The History* said so in episode seven."

"I'm starting to like her," Smith said.

"Look around you," Stan demanded. "You haven't noticed the giant rift above your building?"

"Of course I have, you idiot. That's an experiment the Parallel Universes Division is working on. We have it under control," Werewith said.

The entire room stared at her blankly.

"What, did you think it had anything to do with you? None of you are important to me. Not even you," she said, eyeing Brooks. "We made three more cyborgs this afternoon. Take your conspiracy and stick it where the sun doesn't shine." She paused. "No, don't. You'd like that."

"Wow," Lemon blurted. "You're rude."

As Werewith continued to speak, the rift above the building penetrated the ceiling of her office. "I will show you rude—"

"You don't think *anything* strange is going on here?" Tangelo asked, looking up. "Nothing at all?"

Werewith shook her head, even as the nothingness inched

toward it. "The only strange thing I see happening right now is the fact that you all are still alive, and I've about had it with *that* anomaly."

She picked up the phone, and hovered her finger over the "security" button. Before Security could arrive on the scene and disappoint her, Werewith was suddenly and swiftly drawn into the rift. That was it. One moment she was insulting them; the next she was gone and there was no sign that she'd ever existed. The rift made no sound. They couldn't see her in it. The void turned her to nothing and there wasn't a person in the world who could claim to be upset by that.

What did upset everyone in the room was the fact that the rift was still expanding. They instinctively knelt down and crawled across the room toward its exit as the rift moved lower.

Smith's knees practically screamed at him for the exertion, and he reflected that he should join a gym soon so he could return to his former, only slightly lumpy physique.

"Where do we go now?" Stan asked.

"Parallel Universes?" Brooks suggested. "It's only a semi lead, but it's all we've got."

Smith snorted. "It's not the *only* semi we've got." He was behind Brooks, staring intently at his ass.

"Really?" Brooks asked. "The world is literally ending."

The group scurry-shuffled to the elevator and made its way down. It was fortunate that Agatha Werewith's office was on the third floor and the division they needed was on the fifteenth subfloor. Eighteen floors was a pretty reassuring buffer zone. Of course, if they made it to Parallel Universes and found out they needed to return to a higher floor... well, they all preferred to assume that wouldn't happen.

Reticent elevators weren't meant to hold six people on their hands and knees, so the car was cramped. Once aboard, they all looked up and saw that the emptiness hovered only a foot above their heads. That was a problem since the level it hovered at was about the same level at which the elevator's buttons were located.

"Great," Smith groaned. "Who wants to stick their hand into total nothingness so we can go downstairs?"

"What's even holding the elevator up?" Stan wondered.

"Are there stairs we can take?" Tangelo asked. "That would be preferable to a half-existent elevator car..."

"Agatha Werewith doesn't use *stairs*," Brooks said. She had the third floor stairwell barricaded two years earlier when she became CEO. If the elevator wasn't working, she had reasoned, someone would damn well have to fix it for her, in case of fire or not.

"She doesn't use anything now," Smith laughed.

Stan was fascinated by the void. It was close to the classic physics question. What happened when an unstoppable force (the rift tearing its way through time and space) met an unkillable object (him, Smith, Patience, or Lemon)? What actually happened to people or things that were taken into it? Where was the upper half of this elevator car?

The tear inched lower, and Smith feared for his life for the first time in decades. Brooks clasped his hand, while Patience muttered a little prayer. Lemon and Tangelo shared a glance they hoped wouldn't be their last.

Luckily, someone on a lower floor called for the elevator and it began moving downward. The space between the emptiness and the crouched group grew as they moved from floor to floor. Each of them stood up, barring Smith, whose knees had cramped. He needed a hand from Brooks to stand.

They were standing in half an elevator car, and it made no sense. By all of the laws of the universe, the elevator should no longer be working. The car had no upper half! It had no roof, no cables above it. Stan speculated that it could have something to do with dark matter, but the logistics of it weren't really relevant to their current situation and nobody wanted to hear them.

When the car opened at the third subfloor, a suited group of bigwigs stared at it.

"Is everyone okay upstairs?" one asked.

"Yeah, it's fine," Smith said. "This car's going down, though."

The group of men stared at the one responsible for pressing the button. He turned red, muttered a little "sorry" and pressed the correct button.

"Did you just send those guys upstairs to die?" Lemon asked.

Smith shrugged. "To hell with those guys. Decades of torture here, remember?"

When the car opened at its destination—the seventeenth subfloor—Nicholas Cage stood in the hallway, mouth agape at the half car that greeted him. He cautiously backed away from it, and from the agents who had left him with Reticent guards to be beaten and Nicholas Caged.

"Nicholas Cage?" Stan wondered.

Brooks eyed the intern's badge, still proudly displayed above the waist. "No, that's Jimmy."

"Who?" Smith asked. He didn't remember the unpaid intern whose life he had helped ruin.

"Agent Smith?" Jimmy said. Then came the dig. "You're old and fat."

"And he's a robot," Smith said, gesturing at his partner. "No reason to dwell on it."

"I'm not a robot," Brooks complained.

"It's been *two days*," Jimmy said, blinking.

"Two days ago you didn't look like Nicholas Cage."

Jimmy shrugged. That was a good point. "Is the elevat—"

"Half trapped in another dimension?" Smith finished. "Yeah. I'd take the stairs if I were you."

He heeded his own advice and marched toward the west stairwell that would help them reach the fifteenth subfloor. The group speed-walked through the hallway like they were on a mission to save the world, which they were. If Smith had been the reflecting type, he would have thought about the fact that just a few hours earlier he had wanted the world to end. He would have considered that he never would have seen Brooks again if that had happened, and he would have dedicated himself to the idea that there was always something to live for. He wasn't the reflecting type, though, so mostly he thought about how sore his knees were.

41 / CHAPTER NOT FOUND

Chapter 41 does not exist, which is weird, but this is the setup for a joke that's going to pay off like... five books from now. It's not just for the reference in the next chapter's title...

42 / THE ANSWER TO EVERYTHING

Scientific experiments are delicate things. There are innumerable controls designed to ensure accuracy and relevance. Hypotheses must be testable through careful experimentation. Experiments must be repeatable. Observations lead to new hypotheses, and so on.*

Reticent experiments were not held to such standards. They were not even subject to careful logging. At any given time, dozens of mad scientists did whatever it was they felt they should do with the resources available to them. Oversight was technically there, but as it was in the form of management types who knew nothing about the science their employees were testing, it may as well have not existed. The organization relied on the idea that its employees were reputable human beings, and/or that they were frightened enough of Reticent punishments that they wouldn't do anything to endanger the organization.

It worked, mostly, but one kink in that idea had emerged. If a person were, say, immortal, there could be no consequences. Punishment would have to rely on the idea that the immortal person cared as much about someone else as much as they did about themselves. For instance, to torment Arturo Brooks would be to torment Edward Smith.

That was not the case for Puritan men from 1692. The only thing they cared about was God and displaying their affection toward Him to the most extreme degree possible. There was no way the Reticent could kill God (probably).

---

* For more information, see the "Scientific Method" section of your preferred seventh grade science textbook.

William Stoughton was the worst of those Puritans. He and a recently re-headed John Wilmington sat in a small conference room with two other immortal Puritans: Epenetus Lathrop and Joy-in-Sorrow Noyes. They discussed the progression of their plan.

"Where are we on immortality?" Stoughton asked.

"Not very far," Wilmington replied. "All we were able to get from Patience was that she's immortal. We knew that. We don't know why."

"It's not the time machine?" Lathrop asked.

"No, it's not. Agents Brooks and Smith both used it and only one of them came out immortal. Experiments on Smith haven't yielded anything more than the experiments on the girl."

"With regard to Agent Br—"

"The cybernetic enhancement project is our better bet," Stoughton said.

"Can they survive the void?" Noyes asked.

"We tossed three of them in. Two of those returned. Zero percent of mortals have made it out alive, so that's decidedly better," said Stoughton.

Smith couldn't help himself. He was on the other side of the conference room door with his ear pressed to it when he spouted a loud "what the fuck?"

He realized his volume and decided to roll with it.

"What the fuck?" he repeated, bursting through the door. "Seriously, what the fuck?"

"Agent Smith?" Stoughton was aghast. "You're supposed to be on twenty-six right now. You're also supposed to—"

"I get it," Smith said, exasperated. "I'm supposed to be younger and thinner. *I get it.*"

"I was going to say incapacitated, but yes."

"What's wrong with you?" Brooks asked the religious extremists.

"What's wrong with *us*?" Stoughton repeated. "What's

wrong with you?"

Brooks squinted. "What do you mean?"

"If Christ had not died for thee, thou hadst been damned," Stoughton said.

With those archaic words, some obscure line of code in Brooks's brain triggered him into action. Smith was ready to say something snarky about the lengthy code phrase, but before he got the chance, Brooks grabbed his neck and began strangling him. The good news was that Smith could not die. The bad news was that their strongest ally was now on Team Puritan (Team Pilgrim, as Smith knew it).

Stoughton noticed the small girl tucked at the back of the group. "*Patience Cloyce.*"

"Sir?" she asked. It was the second politest someone had ever been to the person who had ordered their execution. The politest was Atticus Trendoline, an eighteenth century English baker who presented the judge who sentenced him to die with a blackberry pie. The pie, eaten after Trendoline was decapitated, was reported to be delicious, so much so that the judge lamented the sentencing.

"I have to thank you," Stoughton said. "I don't know what you did to grant me eternal life, but I do appreciate it."

"What compels you to destroy everything?" Patience asked. "God created the world and only God should destroy it."

Stoughton sneered. "Your parents always did profess a weak spirituality." Confident they could not be stopped, he explained his evil scheme. "When all of the nonbelievers are gone, it will be a perfect world."

Smith, having been choked to death and tossed aside, awakened and complained. "*That's* your plan? Go buy an island or something. Why would you need to take the entire universe with—" Brooks grabbed his partner's neck again, and Smith's complaint cut off into a gasping sound.

"But it won't be perfect," Lemon corrected. "It's just the

four of you?"

Wilmington nodded, and Stoughton glared at him for answering.

She did some mental math. If Hudson and Stan counted as two separate people (and they sort of did), there were those two, Smith, Brooks, and herself. "There are already more non-Puritan immortals than there are Puritans, then."

"Not once we've amassed our legion," Stoughton corrected. "The cybernetic enhancement project will grow our numbers."

"Seriously?" Lemon asked.

"Who's going to join a Puritan doomsday cult?" Tangelo asked.

Stoughton sighed. "We don't *tell* them it's a Puritan doomsday cult."

Stan looked at Brooks, who was currently choking his partner to death for the third time. It was lucky for Smith that there were no axes in the room.

"They brainwash them," Stan said. "Take any number of people, offer them immortality, then turn them into God's little cybernetic soldiers with the utterance of a passphrase."

"He understands," Noyes said.

"No, I don't," Stan said. "I know what you're doing, but I don't *understand* at all." If he were personally creating a cyborg army, he would turn them into Stormtroopers. Anything else—especially a Puritan cult—just didn't make sense.

Smith, resurrecting for the fourth time, looked up at his partner and had an idea.

"If Christ had not died for thee, thou hadst been damned," he said.

"What?" Brooks asked.

If the phrase had activated him, Smith thought, there was a chance it would deactivate him too. It didn't, but it had been worth a shot. As his partner lunged for him again, Smith tried something else.

"Damned been... hadst thou, thee for died... not had Christ if..." he said.

Brooks backed away.

"That actually worked?" Smith chuckled. He saw Brooks, red-faced and withdrawn, and changed his question to a statement. "That actually worked." He was suddenly proud of himself for having read a bunch of Zatanna comics as a child.*

Brooks looked up and lunged for Stoughton instead.

"If Christ had not—" Noyes started, but Lemon jumped forward and kicked him between the legs before he could finish his words.

"If Christ had—" Lathrop started, but Tangelo mimicked his sister and kicked the man in the groin before he could finish.

"Find something to chop with," Brooks said, and Stan scurried out of the room.

"If Christ had not died for—" Wilmington started, but Patience followed everyone else's lead and kicked him square in the junk before he could finish his words. There was something oddly satisfying about incapacitating the man who had slipped her the noose. She was full of shame, but also glee.

With three Puritans doubled over and groaning, the conference room had taken a turn for the slapstick. Brooks continued to choke Stoughton to death, and Lemon, Tangelo, and Patience each stayed with a hunched down Puritan, feet at the ready. Occasionally one of the men would begin to utter "If Christ had not—" and receive a swift kick to the testicles. They may have been unable to die but they could confirmedly be incapacitated.

Smith, meanwhile, lay on the floor on his back, exhausted. Half a century of doing nothing had taken its toll. He

---

And as an adult.

definitely needed to go to a gym sometime soon. He also needed not to be choked to death anytime soon.

Stan scurried back into the room, toting a broadsword that he'd grabbed from a janitor's closet. He didn't concern himself with why there was a broadsword in the janitor's closet because, frankly, it had been a long day and that was nowhere near the strangest part of it. He handed it off to Brooks, who swiftly decapitated William Stoughton. That thrilled Patience, which in turn made her feel ashamed.

Brooks tossed the head to his partner, then moved along to Noyes. With a swift chop, his head was also gone. Brooks handed it to Lemon, with instructions. "Keep this away from his body." She nodded.

Tangelo glanced at his sister holding a man's severed head and decided that, yes, she actually was a grown-up and, yes, she would be okay. Brooks repeated the maneuver on Lathrop, and handed Tangelo that Puritan's head. He was more disturbed than his sister had been, but decided that he had to get over it if he was going to return to the future. He would, after all, see a lot worse defending space after he was conscripted.

"How do we get rid of the rift?" Brooks asked the last Puritan as he held the sword to his neck.

John Wilmington was, like most Puritans, full of contempt, and he refused to answer. "You'll have to cut off my—"

Brooks obliged, and tossed that head to Stan, deciding against inflicting it on Patience. She was slightly disappointed, and more than slightly ashamed at having been slightly disappointed.

"Not that I'm not glad those assholes are gone," Smith said, "but what are we supposed to do now?"

"We need to find where they're generating the rift," Stan said. "This is the Parallel Universes floor, right? It should be nearby..."

"Yeah, well there's no Division of Giant Gashes in Space-

Time on the directory," Smith said.

"Then we'll have to search everything," Stan said.

"What are we supposed to do with these?" Tangelo asked, holding the severed head as far from his body as possible.

Brooks looked around, then noted the escape hatch at the side of the room. In case of an emergency, the conference room was equipped to expel its occupants back above ground a few blocks from Reticent headquarters. "Here," he said. "Toss them in here."

"You don't think a pile of severed heads on a Manhattan sidewalk will draw the attention of the police?" Smith asked.

"They'll notice. That's the idea," Brooks said. "Sort of. It will give the Reticent something else to focus on and clear this floor for us. Plus the heads will be nowhere near the bodies." He gestured at the hatch. "Toss them."

"Okay," Smith said, "but heads are gonna roll for this."

Brooks just shook his head.

Each member of the group disposed of the heads as they had been instructed.

43 / THAT KIND OF DAY

There are some things that can ruin a person's day: stepping in dog poop, receiving the wrong order at a drive-thru and only realizing it miles down the road, being forced to engage in conversation with someone who does CrossFit... any of those things lets the person experiencing it know that it's going to be *that* kind of day.

All of those paled in comparison to finding four bodiless heads on the sidewalk, which is exactly what happened to Trissa Johnson. After she finished screaming, she decided she was obligated to call the police. When she thought about how late for work that would make her, she was furious. This was going to be *that* kind of day.

"Seriously?" she muttered to herself. "What kind of half-assed serial killer just leaves his work on the damn sidewalk?" She had half a mind to find the killer and berate him herself.

Reticent alerts went off when the escape hatch was used, and Reticent agents subsequently tried to reach Trissa before she could call the police. They failed, and Trissa was soon joined by a crowd of tourists gawking at the macabre display. A Japanese couple readied a selfie stick and leaned in for a picture; this was the second most exciting thing they had seen on their trip, the first being the giant rift above Manhattan. New York natives saw that Trissa had the situation handled and kept walking, picking up their paces and thanking whichever deities they did or didn't believe in that they weren't the first to come across the scene. It wasn't going to be *that* kind of day for them.

44 / BURN, BABY, BURN

Back inside, the alarms sang. TWINKLE TING TWINKLE TWINKLE TING. A voice came over the intercom. "This is a routine drill. Repeat: this is a routine drill." What that meant was that everyone in the building was to hide whatever strange cases they were working and pretend they were working on something routine. Each agent had a backup folder containing drug trial research, consumer complaints, and other unsuspicious items. Areas that were obviously suspicious, like the medical experimentation labs, were closed off so that the doors appeared to be normal walls. Lab workers began checking normal human DNA instead of werewolf or vampire samples, which they locked away. Everyone had gotten good at the drill since it happened at least a few times per year.

The scientists who were working on transmitting a gateway to a parallel universe turned their machine off, and the rift disappeared. They replaced their work with the perfectly normal experiment of treating cancerous tumors with a shrink ray.

"Well," Brooks said, "that's one way to take care of it."

"They'll bring it back as soon as the drill is over. Idiots probably have no idea what they're doing."

"I have an idea," Tangelo said. "Burn it down."

"There are innocent people in here," Stan said. "I guess."

"Then pull the fire alarm, and *then* burn it down. It worked on your house."

Brooks and Smith looked at each other, considering that. A fire wouldn't penetrate every area of the building, but it would get the place shut down for renovations.

"If we warn the people on this floor," Smith said, "they'll come back and do it again as soon as the Reticent rebuilds."

"Are you saying you want to let them burn to death?" Lemon asked, horrified.

"Want to? No. I'm being practical. We don't want to be in this exact scenario in a few months."

"We may not have to kill them," Brooks said. "Once the chaos clears they'll realize Werewith is gone and the whole company will have to reorganize."

Smith didn't follow. "So?"

"So not too many people know we fucked them over," Brooks said. "Werewith: dead. Nguyen: dead. Marsh: dead. The board: super dead. A whole lot more people know about the Goblin King..."

"You want to take it over?" Smith asked, articulating what his partner had insinuated.

"We could literally run the place forever," Brooks said. "Make it what it was supposed to be."

Smith took the opportunity to tease him. "But you'll never get the chance to use that 401k you love so much."

Brooks rolled his eyes. "I said 'could,' not 'will.' One problem, though. The sprinkler system."

"Oh, I can take care of that one," Smith said. "Burroughs owes me a favor."

"Still?" Brooks wondered, certain that Smith had used that favor on at least four separate occasions.

"No, this one's a new favor." Smith simultaneously shrugged and winked, then proceeded to call his former partner. "Yeah, hi. You're a computer genius," he said. "I'm not looking for revenge porn... No. Yes. No. No. No. I need another favor." A pause. "Because you stabbed my partner to death. Yeah. I got better. Yeah. He got better too. Don't apologize, just do me a favor." Another pause. "What do you know about the sprinkler system?" A long pause. "Well, I need you to disable it."

Five minutes later, the system was disabled. Tangelo pulled the fire alarm, and floor by floor the halls and offices cleared out. Stan walked their little group to the janitor's closet where he'd previously found a broadsword and directed them to the several gallons of gasoline sitting on a shelf. None of them wondered why there were dozens of gallons of gasoline on a shelf in a janitor's closet. It had been *that* kind of day.

They roamed the halls, spraying gasoline haphazardly and gradually making their way upstairs. When it came time to light the blaze, the group took the front door out of the building. Employees used a different entrance and this minimized the number of Reticent agents who would see what was about to happen. Tangelo was the first out of the building. Once the mortal Lunan stood a safe distance away, Smith flicked his skull-shaped lighter and tossed it into the building. Thanks to nonexistent fire codes at the time of its construction, the Victorian building that housed Reticent headquarters' aboveground facilities immediately went up in flames.

Police sirens grew louder and closer on account of the sidewalk decapitations. Officer Tomas Ramirez, the first on the scene, stepped out of his vehicle at the same moment the building went up. He sighed, got back into his car, and called the fire department. Was it really an emergency? He thought so, but the woman on the other end of the line disagreed. All units were busy trying to figure out what had happened to everything above the third floor—not of Reticent headquarters but of a substantial portion of the Lower East Side.

It was for that reason the building was left to burn.

45 / DRUNK TANK

While the day had only lasted the standard twenty-four hours, it had felt a lot longer. Brooks, Smith, Stan, Tangelo, Lemon, and Patience (with her own newly acquired fake ID) parked the time machine in the remnants of the Brooks/Smith brownstone and filed into Pucker Up for post-saving-the-universe refreshments. Stan, Brooks, Tangelo, and Lemon (to her brother's chagrin) tried the bar's signature cocktail: Lemony Chicot's Series of Fortunate Ferments. Patience ordered a water, impressed that it was guaranteed to be clean and potable. Smith sampled the Mangerine Twist, which raised a concern.

"Should you be drinking?" Brooks asked.

Smith stared at him. "Why wouldn't I be?"

"Because you're an alcoholic," Brooks noted.

Smith's eyes shifted from side to side before resettling. "I'm also immortal."

"I don't think that makes addiction not a problem."

"Yeah, it does," Smith said.

"I don't think it does."

"It definitely does." Smith turned to Stan. "What do you think?"

"I think I'm staying out of this," Stan said.

Lemon walked across the bar to her favorite jukebox. It was the only Earthly jukebox she'd ever seen, which made it her favorite. Each page was littered with old favorites, songs that were impossible to acquire legally on the moon. She pressed something by the Shins and remembered her mother humming their music to her when she was younger. Lemon sighed as she returned to the table.

"It's about time we got back to the future," Stan said. "Don't you think?"

Tangelo nodded. Lemon sighed again, more pointedly.

"I don't wanna go back," she complained, remembering her Twitter followers and an irrelevant adventure through a record store with Duke.

"Well, you have to," Tangelo insisted.

"Why?" she asked.

"Tell her," Tangelo said, looking at Stan.

"Strictly speaking, she doesn't have to. If she were to choose to stay here, that's the course she's always taken, and..." Stan realized too late that Tangelo didn't want the truth. "Oh, yes. She has to go back to the future because, uh... physics."

Lemon crossed her arms. "See?"

"Lemon." Tangelo's voice was stern. "You can't stay in the past because of some boy."

"It's not because of Duke," she insisted.

Smith spit out a bit of his drink. "*Duke*? You want to reject two hundred years of technology for a guy named *Duke*?"

"For the last time, it's *not* the guy. It's the chance to live in history. It's being somewhere totally different. I'd never seen a tree before yesterday! There are only 600,000 people on the entire moon. There are nine million in this city alone!" She thought about the number of obscure bands she could see live, the number of locally sourced creations she could try. The past was her future. It had to be.

Tangelo remembered the look on his sister's face when she was handed a decapitated head. In that moment, his younger sister was no longer his kid sister.

"You know what?" he said. "You're seventeen. If this is really what you want to do..."

Lemon's eyes lit up. "Seriously?" She hugged her brother. "We can send each other postcards through time like in *The Lake House*!"

"People watch *The Lake House* in two hundred years?" Brooks wondered.

"No," Tangelo assured them. "Not normal people. Just her."

"We'll look out for your sister," Smith said.

His partner's jaw dropped. "Are... are you serious?" It had never occurred to him that Smith would ever, in a million years, volunteer to look after a teenager.

"What?" Smith shrugged. "I like her. She puked. Besides, I told you a few things had changed in seventy years..."

"Does that mean what I think it does?" Brooks asked.

Smith glanced at Patience. "I'm saying a couple of immortal guys could do worse than taking in a couple of immortal teenagers."

"We still don't actually know I'm immortal," Brooks said.

"We'll live the same amount of time one way or another."

"*Wow*. Dark," Brooks said.

"Is that an invitation to live with you, sirs?" Patience asked.

Smith smirked. "Only if you stop saying 'sir,' goddamnit."

Patience gasped.

"Stop that," Brooks demanded.

Smith shrugged. "I haven't changed *that* much."

"We're gonna get out of here," Stan said, standing with Tangelo. "If you ever need a time machine, you know where to find it."

Brooks and Smith nodded. Lemon stood and squeezed her brother tight.

"I'll see you around," she said. "Look for my letters!"

Tangelo knew she meant it, and he knew he didn't have to worry about her. He and Stan returned to the machine and, eventually, to the year 2202, where an intact Luna awaited.

"Let's go home," Brooks said.

"Your house burned down," Lemon pointed out.

Brooks changed his mind. "Let's... go get some hotel rooms."

"What's a hotel?" Patience asked.

"An inn," Brooks said.

She nodded, comprehending that word.

"You've got a lot to learn, pilgrim," Smith said, tapping her on the shoulder.

"I'm a Puritan, sir," Patience corrected.

"God damn it."

She gasped.

46 / MEET THE NEW BOSSES

A few weeks later, Brooks and Smith sat in the first subfloor conference room. It was the only floor at the moment. There had been many conference rooms but this was now *the* conference room while the organization rebuilt its facilities. Reticent Headquarters was going to join modern Manhattan. No longer would it be three stories of eighteenth century masterwork with secrets below; it would be a skyscraper, the first in its neighborhood after the Six Block Disaster.

CEO Arturo Brooks presented building plans that maintained the organization's facade without being suspicious in any way. President Edward Smith made sure the organization's agents were advised of and approved this direction. He had wanted Brooks to act as both the President and CEO, but a suspicious clause in the Reticent Code directed that at no time could any 'robots or other cybernetically enhanced beings' hold the position of President.

So it went that Brooks made business decisions and Smith worked the organization's markedly less seedy underbelly. Policy changes included a strict No Parallel Universes order, and a directive that there would no longer be, under any circumstances, human experimentation or torture (vampires and the like were still fair game). The two men discussed this policy over drinks. Brooks still objected to his partner's drinking, but he couldn't yet mount a successful argument against an immortal man.

"What are we going to do about you?" Brooks asked. "Past you."

Past Smith still lay tied to a cot in one of the aforementioned sections of the building that did not burn, not being tortured.

"If you free me, you always freed me, right? So it doesn't

work—"

"Or you thought you were captive a lot longer than you were," Brooks pointed out.

Smith rolled his eyes. "How the hell would that happen?"

Brooks stared pointedly at the Scotch in Smith's hand.

"Come on."

"Only one way to find out," said Brooks.

Within the hour, the 2014 version of Smith was freed from captivity. He exited from the manhole cover at the end of an emergency exit pathway and found that the building had burned to the ground. From a distance, the President and CEO observed him through binoculars. They also had him bugged before his release, and they shared a set of head-phones to hear anything he had to say. It wasn't Presidential or CEO-ial behavior, but they were new at this and they couldn't help themselves. They were, after all, detectives at heart.

The younger Smith stumbled down the sidewalk across the street from the building. He tripped over a stray ear that had somehow ended up on the sidewalk and fell to the ground.

"I can't help that," Smith said. "They drugged me. You can't hold that against me."

They watched as the young version looked over, confused, at the construction zone that had once held Reticent head-quarters. "What the hell?" he said. "What year is it?"

"That's a fair question," Smith insisted.

The younger Smith observed his surroundings. They were familiar but different. Across the street, in the building that once housed MacGuffin's, his favorite lunch stop, was a new restaurant. Its neon green Helvetica sign boasted a preten-tious name: 2045.

"2045?" the younger Smith muttered, taking in that he had been held captive for thirty years.

"Oh, fuck," the older Smith said.

"That restaurant went up last week," Brooks said. Then he

laughed. "You thought three weeks of torture was thirty years because of a burger joint."

"I did." Smith almost couldn't believe it. "I fucking did."

"So how big a bender did you go on afterward that you never figured out the *year*?"

"Yeah, okay." Smith took his flask and dumped it out on the ground. "Fine."

His younger self stumbled off into the sunset to get absolutely plastered.

47 / KALE

A month later, Smith looked down at his packed lunch with disdain. He was a man's man, damn it—a man's man who swore and repressed his feelings to the best of his ability. And there was one thing he knew about men's men: they did not eat salad for lunch. But there he was, pressing his fork into vegetables. The kale wasn't the only thing that was bitter, and Smith mumbled something explicit.

"If you hate it so much, don't eat it," Brooks said, coming up from a bite of his sandwich. "You know I don't care." He actually kind of liked Smith's extra fluff.

"I'm torn," said Smith. "I have too much self-respect to eat kale, but I also have too much self-respect to keep looking like Hudson Marrow."

As if on cue, a voice came from the doorway.

"Thanks," Hudson said. "That really boosts my post-divorce confidence."

Smith backtracked. "Not you. You look great. I mean future you."

"Uh huh." Hudson eyed the giant stacks of paper all over the room. "You guys busy?"

"Yep," Brooks said. "Divorce, though? The thing didn't work out?"

"The thing where I chased my estranged, immortal wife to Texas and tried to win her back with the promise of money in lieu of real companionship?"

Brooks shrugged.

"No, that thing didn't work," Hudson said. "I did, however, get a list of everyone who bought something at the yard sale." Veronica's record keeping was truly impressive, but that probably should have been expected from a tax accountant.

"Really? Everyone?"

"Oh yeah," Hudson said. "Did I ever mention the financial records she pulled out for the divorce?"

"No," Smith said. "Probably because we're not friends."

"In any case, she had me tracked down to the last convenience store burrito," Hudson said.

"God, that sounds amazing right now," Smith said.

Brooks shook his head and mouthed "no."

"Anyway," Hudson said, "I retrieved all of the artifacts. Only about forty percent of the buyers ended up being immortal, and now they can't pass it on, so—"

"Unless one of them also invents time machine," Brooks said, adding a caveat.

"Yeah... unless that happens." Hudson continued. "I was going to return everything to its rightful place in history, but decided it might be bad if Attila the Hun or Hitler suddenly became immortal."

"So what did you do with it?" Smith asked.

"I hid it all in a bunker."

"You have a bunker?" Brooks wondered. "You live in an apartment."

"I had one custom built. It's in the middle of nowhere in Texas. Well, it *was* the middle of nowhere. Now they're going to build a Chipotle on top of it."

Smith groaned. If a convenience store burrito sounded amazing, a Chipotle burrito was the culinary equivalent of an orgasm. Brooks patted him on the shoulder.

"You want a job?" Brooks asked Hudson.

"Excuse me?"

"We didn't ask you to come here to talk about the yard sale. You were smart enough to invent a time machine and you're working in rock fraud," said Brooks.

"I'm not entirely clear what your organization does," Hudson said.

Smith laughed. "Neither are we."

"Whatever you want to do," Brooks said. "Really."

"Yes." Hudson spoke before his mind had agreed. "One condition, though."

"What?"

"You can't ask me to use the time machine again. All it did was cause a giant mess."

"Hey, I wouldn't be here without it," Smith said.

"I'll still use it in the future," Hudson said. "Stan will still come visit you. But other than that, let's just... not. Okay?"

"Of course," Brooks said. "We don't want anything to do with it either."

Brooks shook Hudson's hand.

"I look forward to what you come up with next," he said.

Smith shook his hand as well. "I look forward to learning more about whether the marble in the lobby really is marble after all..."

48 / UNPLANNED PARENTHOOD

Refurbishing a half-burnt brownstone was not cheap, especially when Brooks and Smith's homeowner's insurance refused to pay out. The company blamed the fire—and most other claims in the city that had happened the week of the Six Block Disaster—on the rift. And inter-dimensional tears, they explained, were not covered. Luckily, despite budget cuts the President and CEO of the Reticent still made an obscene amount of money. It actually upset Brooks and Smith how obscene the amount of money was, but it didn't upset them enough that they would lower their own salaries. That would just be stupid.

The pair sat in their living room, playing a brand new copy of the board game LIFE with Patience. Lemon was busy with more digital pursuits.

"I don't see how having two kids makes you a winner," Smith said. "Do they know how much teenagers eat?"

"That's just how the game works," Brooks said.

Smith took a sip of water, then glared at the glass for not containing whiskey. "Can I trade my kid for money?"

"What? *No.*"

"How do I even have a kid? I married a dude. Is this some sort of Conner Kent thing?"

Brooks blinked. "I have no idea what you're talking about."

"Superboy. Come on."

"You're mad because you're losing," teased Brooks.

"I'm not mad, I'm annoyed. I'm annoyed because this game is *stupid*," Smith said.

"What would you prefer we play?"

"I'd prefer we *fore*play."

"Oh-ho!" Lemon looked up from her phone and shouted

from the kitchen. She quickly lost interest and resumed texting Duke.

"I hate you," Brooks declared. "I actually hate you." He refused to smile as he moved his plastic car to the end of the board. "Also, I just won."

Smith groaned. "Goddamn it."

Patience had run out of gasps, but she did show a tinge of discomfort. Brooks elbowed his partner to alert him to his mistake; in response, Smith rolled his eyes and let out an almost silent "sorry."

"I enjoyed that game," Patience declared. "Are there others?"

"Cards Against Humanity?" Smith offered.

Brooks dismissed the adult party game with a curt "No."

Smith grunted with displeasure. "I'm hungry. Order in?"

"I think you've had enough," Brooks said, poking at his partner's stomach.

"This is what it's come to," Smith said. "I suffer a century of trauma and I'm just a walking fat joke to you."

"You're not *just* a fat joke," Brooks said.

"I've never seen you go for a walk," Patience said.

"Oh-ho!" came another shout from the kitchen.

Smith cursed under his breath.

The evening continued in that vein, as did the evening after and the evening after that. Fat jokes aside, the tension that had been building for years was gone. It's not that everything was great or that everything would ever be great (how great could being a cyborg ever be?), but everything was okay, and that was okay enough.

APPENDIX I / RETICENT CODES

The Reticent New Employee Handbook outlines 43 potentially apocalyptic scenarios and how to handle them. As events become obsolete they are replaced within the code by new ones, so numbering should not be considered to indicate any order of importance. The events are listed below, but the procedures for dealing with them are, unfortunately, classified.

1. Biblical Plagues
2. The Rapture
3. Zombie Virus
4. Non-Zombie Virus
5. Mass Insanity
6. Alien Invasion
7. Killer Robots
8. Genetically-Altered Superhumans
9. Mass Infertility
10. Nuclear Disaster
11. Asteroid Impact(s)
12. Genie(s)
13. Supervolcano
14. Successful Time Travel
15. Angels and/or Demons
16. Unspecified Giant Monster (e.g., Cthulhu)
17. Wizard Battle
18. Multiverse Conflict
19. Evil Dolls, Mass Production
20. Mass Poisoning
21. Global Flood
22. Supernova

23. Nazi Invasion*
24. Witch Alliance
25. Newly Sentient Animals
26. Suddenly Prevalent Allergy
27. Polar Shift
28. Overpopulation
29. Terrorist Attack
30. Large Hadron Collider
31. Gamma Radiation
32. Mayan Prophecy
33. Non-Mayan Prophecy
34. Human Devolution
35. Honeybees, Disappearance of
36. Bath Salts
37. Ultimate Fate of the Universe (Unknown)
38. Life is a Simulation
39. Leprechauns
40. Loss of Moon
41. Nanobots
42. Earth Bulldozed for Intergalactic Superhighway
43. Other†

---

* Nazis were added to the Reticent codes in 1939. While they may not seem relevant today, the code was left in the handbook just in case.

† Code 43 has historically been abused by agents trying to make their assignments seem more important than they are.

APPENDIX II / CLOYCE FAMILY TREE

Because fantasy readers love useless information...

BARTHOLOMEW CLOYCE – Fisherman, Age 54
PRUDENCE CLOYCE – His Wife, Age 50
Their Children:
DAMARIS EDWARDS (née CLOYCE) – 33
    JONATHAN EDWARDS – Her Husband, 38
    Their Children:
        REJOICE EDWARDS, 17
        CONSTANCE EDWARDS, 14
        HEZEKIAH EDWARDS, 12
        KATHERINE EDWARDS, 8
        EDWARD EDWARDS, Deceased
        EDWARD EDWARDS II, 4
        ISAAC EDWARDS, 1
ZACHARIAH CLOYCE – 30
    PEREGRINE CLOYCE (née HEYRICK) – His Wife, Deceased
    Their Children:
        CHRISTOPHER CLOYCE, 7
        PETER CLOYCE, 3
EDWARD CLOYCE – 29
    MARY CLOYCE (née HEYRICK) – His Wife, 25
    Their Children:
        ROBERT CLOYCE, 8
        REMEMBER CLOYCE, 4
        HUMILITY CLOYCE, 4
        JOAN CLOYCE, 2

FAITH MOORE (née CLOYCE) – 26
    THOMAS MOORE – Her Husband, 30
    Their Children:
        SUSANNA MOORE, 6
        FRANCIS MOORE, 5
        JASPER MOORE, 3
        RICHARD MOORE, 2
RESOLVE COOKE (née CLOYCE) – 24
    THOMAS COOKE – Her Husband, 30
    Their Children:
        PATIENCE COOKE, 5
        THOMAS COOKE, 1
EZEKIEL CLOYCE – 22
    ELIZABETH CLOYCE (née RICE) – His Wife, 18
    Their Children:
        HUNTER CLOYCE, 3
        JACOB CLOYCE, 1
ISABELLA ABBOTT (née CLOYCE) – 18
    MUCH-IN-HAND ABBOTT – Her Husband, 40
PATIENCE CLOYCE – 15
NATHAN CLOYCE – 7

ACKNOWLEDGEMENTS

This is a book. If it weren't for my mom reading to me every night when I was little, I might not know what a book is, so I thank her. I thank my sisters for being rowdy little shits who made me retreat to my room and write stories. I thank my lucky stars I was born early enough that those stories aren't online. I thank Katherine and Shane for checking my work. I thank fellow netizens Liannabob and Defne for acting as beta readers and sounding boards. There's nothing quite like receiving a furious email with the subject line "WHAT THE HELL [SPOILER] DIED?" at 2AM on a weekday. Ellen Campbell edited this and reminded me of important things like the difference between hoard and horde. I thank her.

Finally, thank YOU for reading. If this book gave you a chuckle or two, drop a review on Amazon or Goodreads so the algorithm knows you'd like more content like it. We live in a dystopia where that sort of thing matters.

Brooks and Smith return in:
Time Purge (Book 2)
A Genie Ruins Everything (Book 3)
Fun Times in a Dystopic Hellscape (Book 4)

Also from the Author:
The Bedazzlers

For announcements about new projects,
sign up for the mailing list at martina-fetzer.com, or
scan this little QR code...

Made in the USA
Monee, IL
11 March 2023